DISTANT HILLS

LYDIA UNSWORTH

ATLATL

Atlatl Press
POB 521
Dayton, Ohio 45401
atlatlpress.com
info@atlatlpress.com

Distant Hills
Copyright © 2020 by Lydia Unsworth
Cover design copyright © 2020 by Squidbar Designs
ISBN-13: 978-1-941918-73-9

This book is a work of fiction. Names, characters, business organizations, places, events, and incidents either are the product of the author's imagination or are used fictitiously. The author's use of names of actual persons (living or dead), places, and characters is incidental to the purposes of the plot, and is not intended to change the entirely fictional character of the work.

No part of this work may be reproduced, stored in a retrieval system, or transmitted by any means without the written permission of the author or publisher.

For Adrian

Also by Lydia Unsworth

Certain Manoeuvres
Nostalgia for Bodies
Yield
I Have Not Led a Serious Life

DISTANT HILLS

if you are alone, you are wholly your own
— Leonardo da Vinci

no you without mountains, without sun, without sky
— Rebecca Solnit

"And people in their Sunday best
Stroll about, swaying over the gravel
Under this enormous sky
Which, from hills in the distance,
Stretches to distant hills."

—Franz Kafka, "Description of a Struggle"

DISTANT HILLS

loosely open for an answer.

'Oh, right. I don't know. The day after tomorrow, I suppose. It's Wednesday, today? Yeah. Then, Friday.'

'That's come around fast. Feels like you've only been back a few weeks.'

'I have only been back a few weeks.'

'Right.'

Kathy pulls the handles of her bag apart and shuffles inside, brings a few items up for a moment, or maybe the same item repeatedly, but not beyond the rim of the bag, not so I can see. There are fourteen low-hanging ceiling lights in this cafe, each comprising one long wire with an under-lit UFO thing hovering off the end, and eight spotlights behind the bar. It rains. Lines of stretched-out drops thin as a photo-booth pencil-drawing portrait. I want to go home and consider the night sky. Just lie flat out against a cold surface and try to think my way into a reversal, making up feel like down. I don't want to go anywhere until it stops raining. It stops.

Kathy big-exhales and warm-smiles like she's been here an hour already. Two hands on the bag handles, I notice. She is sat almost 100% upright and about mid-way towards the front of the chair. Not quite a perch, but could steal into one at a moment's warning. The rain turns our heads. *It's coming down again*, Kathy says, and relaxes a little. Different kind of exhalation now, less anticipation in it, more like she's given herself over to the next few thousand seconds. There will be no more battles with that time.

'How are the kids?' I ask.

And I don't hear the answer but probably it's fine. She starts telling me about a recent parents' evening and some new kid mediation class in the area, and this vase that was smashed—was it in a relative's house or a shop?—I missed a few of the details and then I couldn't ask because she'd start from the beginning again and I'm not sure how long ago that was and I don't want her to think bad of me and I love watching her face like this; it goes up and down and there's joy in the waves. I want to grab her and scream and be nine years old and have the whole world spinning around us but I don't and we're not and it doesn't. The colour of the coffee is close to perfection. It is exactly the same every single time and that in itself has got to be some kind of miracle. It is not even a colour I particularly like, it is only that I know it, it's constant.

'So, you should come over,' she says, 'before you go.'

'Yeah, sure. When?'

'How about tonight? We have a couple of friends coming round for dinner anyway. I'm sure there'll be enough for one more. Say, eight-ish?'

'Yeah, right okay, yeah. Sorry, I'm a bit . . . you know. It's early and I'm sure there's something I forgot to do yesterday only I can't figure out what it is. Anyway, I'll have a couple more of these (slaps side of coffee cup) and I'm sure I'll be more lively later (raised-eyebrow smile with you-know-me expression).'

'Oh, don't worry about it. Look, I've got to get off, there's a couple of things I need to return. Kids' stuff, you know (eyeball roll and faux-hardship smile).'

But I don't. I don't know what she's talking about. I smile and nod and wave and we were thirteen years old once, drinking two-litre bottles of cider on a wet field, laughing and crying and squatting down with skinny jeans pulled between our half-formed ankles, trying not to fall over or piss on our shoes but a little bit wanting to so we could laugh about it later and remember.

DISTANT HILLS

I am holding a bottle of wine between hot fingers. Trying to hold it as nonchalantly as possible, as if about to swing it upwards and take a gulp. It feels good holding it like that. It's a Zinfandel. I have decided Zinfandels and Pinot grigios are my favourites because it is important to have substance, to have answers for people's questions, in order to keep the conversation fluid, and to learn more from the exchange. People rarely like to teach true novices. It's better to know a little and have them think they're an expert teaching an enthusiast rather than have them think you're a completely different sort. Then it's just a matter of nodding until the unusually specific adjectives start to become familiar. The wine is a Zinfandel, and today I chose one from California because I've been thinking about whale migrations a lot recently and the bottle's label matched the name of a friend.

The Zinfandel was £8.15, reduced to £4.99, which I thought an acceptable standard for the occasion. I might not get a knowing glance, but hopefully it'll be taken as mid-range and slipped in among the other bottles like unestranged family, without interrupting the flow. An arm movement between words. A swoop parallel with a phrase.

It is still raining lightly and my fringe is shrinking into itself, curling me into a shier version of my usual aplomb. The version that shoves its hands into its hair-roots and jostles them too often in lieu of actual volume. Because it is important to have substance.

I wasn't going to come tonight but then I was and then I wasn't and it becomes impossible once it reaches that point to remember with which opinion one started, to know the real me. It is impossible to trace it back due to the subtle distortions of memory and our ability to place retroactive interpretations on things. The past as well as the future is changing, always—like a universe that can't keep still, sitting in its chair but wriggling constantly, talking over you and going on and on. I decided to come because if you don't you can't imagine what you are missing whereas it is very easy to imagine sitting at home trying to imagine what you might be missing by failing to come. Still, I'm not there yet and anything could happen.

I could drink this wine and rip my clothes off and run into the oncoming traffic. I would probably be quite charming after the initial shock, convincing whoever stopped to reclothe me that I simply wanted to be free and was testing the boundaries of public space and all that. They would probably take me home for coffee and water having first shielded me from nearby mental perversions with their L-size vintage-shop leather jacket. My life would probably be changed right there, meeting someone so removed from any link to any other links in my pre-existing social chains. We might move to Swansea to run a small business together and when customers asked about how we met we'd leave out the exact quantity of Zinfandel and the fact that I was undressed. And every Sunday we'd drive to the ocean to remember our former lives and think about the spaces between things.

My fringe is stuck flat against my forehead, the wetness of my hair making my whole appearance limp. It's not that I mind too much but it's hard to tell a good story, to really get the audience behind you, when it looks like you've just forgotten to be neat. When you think you can hear them wondering if *you* think you made an effort tonight. Without the rain's intervention, at least that much is clear; I'm either this or I'm that, and they'll see that I appear to be okay whichever. Now, post-rain, they won't be sure, they'll be looking for clues. The difficulty lies in the fact I can see them thinking it, trying to locate me. But they need to dry me out first.

The sun is at that angle where you want to baby-talk at it to see if you can make it do something. You could just not go. Kathy isn't going to notice you are not there for another hour or more, and by the time she has she'll have forgotten again. You can only have seen each other four times this year; twice in one day seems a bit OTT. And the babies will be sleeping, so it's not like it will add anything to their experience of the world. The evening will only result in your drinking too much because you don't know where to put your hands or how else to stop your swinging mouth. Taking the edges off your words and letting them all slide out together. A pink face trying to chase itself. Eyes losing their grip of surfaces. Your not going will affect nobody.

'Hi!' Kathy sings as the door spins open, holding that syllable until it dissolves into the sea. 'Glad you could make it. We were about to eat. Weren't sure if you were going to—have you met Mona? I can't remember. She's here with Dean. Dean's here, by the way. Up visiting family. The kids are asleep, you just missed them. We didn't know if—what time you would come. How did you get here? Do you need to stay over? It's fine, we can pull the spare bed out. Mona and Dean are staying in the guest room. I could have lumped the kids in together if I'd thought. Do you want something to drink? Oh, Zinfandel, nice. Come in!'

There they are, the three of them, with their bodies. Rocking to and fro like three giddy metronomes. I laugh as I enter the room, so they'll think I'm already a part of it. I try not to sit opposite Dean but end up directly opposite him.

'Hi.' (him)
    'Hi.' (me)
    He introduces me to Mona. I tell him we've already met. He asks where/when? I tell him it was when we all got together before Christmas. He doubts me. She doesn't remember. I tell her (and him) that usually it is me who remembers. I remember her face. We didn't talk much; we weren't sat together. A few sentences perhaps. It is just that I remember. We introduce ourselves again, properly. Mr. Kathy tops up my glass and I note, impressed, that I have managed to kill half an introductory wine without even being told I was clutching it.
    It's a long, long life and I wonder how many times I have done this. Making eye contact, avoiding eye contact, raising glasses, raising glasses. Dean's fucking face. I don't want it opposite me. Looking for whatever it is that it is looking for. Trying to get me to acquiesce into some kind of shared history or whatever. To nod my way into his personal life story; sign some boxes with a brow-raise. To say, yes, you can have that, use it, move it around. We can talk about it if you want, over a cocktail or two in the corner of an amber-lit room. We'll keep thinking of things to say before the glasses reach our lips: salt around the rim crystallising. Laughing like adults about sexual forays and how trite we all are. You will have no darkness in the crease of your collar, Dean, and I will no longer bite my nails. Real people. £10 a drink. Embossed toilet paper. Chrome.
    Mr. Kathy is talking to me now, teasing me about something I

DISTANT HILLS

did a decade ago because he doesn't know me anymore. I look at Dean's mouth but not his eyes. I don't want the lock. He can't know me. He can't be any closer than this. He can have the stories I give him and nothing more; the image I have chosen for him, based on change. My face is friendly, yet unsearchable. Highlighting how little we have in common. Frosted glass. A musical mobile hanging over a baby's cot: you can't discuss things with that. I don't want to discuss things with Dean. Don't want to help him in his Deanness. To add gravity to when he shakes somebody's hand and says, 'Hi, I'm Dean.' I don't want any part of it. I stare at Dean's mouth, only flicking up to his eyes when I want to see a reaction. His face is littered with freckles. Funny things. How they have their place.

The size of how much Mr. Kathy needs someone to laugh at his joke starts to demand an answer. I jolt up and do what he needs. Kathy is here now too, sitting. We are all sitting. Spines at the ready. Hooks in our necks. Designing our own old age. Like ferns folding back in again.

'I'm moving to Croatia,' I say, before I say 'three months' because they keep asking how long I have known him.

I was hitchhiking all summer, trying to be a person who didn't need anything. Out late, up early, at the side of the road for most of the morning, running back and forth to petrol stations to put coffee in, to let coffee out again. He bought two onions in the supermarket. First picked up one, then ran back for the second, said he didn't want the first to be lonely. I was speaking so quickly. There isn't enough time in the world to make another person understand, much less when you only have an evening. We were eating ice cream in the car he had been driving, badly, on what we would call an A-road, overlooking what they would call a *rijeka*. The lights of the city; electronic mesh on the valleys. Old castle walls weaving in and out of the recent future. The wrong side of familiar. Nerves making me more electric. Fuzzy electron clouds. I'll do anything to feel free. We swooped down the hill and through and around. The city's shape playful, launching at us from all angles. The voices of seventies rock idols and the wild wind on a boat filled with people who didn't know where I was from, and the drinks that made it all congeal. The allure of unmemory. A braver dream. Salted eggs on thick brown bread. Why wouldn't I let that happen? Why wouldn't I throw myself in?

They are looking at me like this is the only time I have decided to do something radical and I'm losing respect for them for believing in me. For allowing me to distract them from their own crushing solitude. I don't want to swap travel stories or compare phone tariffs or mortgage deposits. I want to know why they haven't killed themselves yet. For what reason are these four people still alive? It's one of the reasons I drink, to get other people drunk enough to stop pretending. I want us all to cry, because only then can we start to make good things happen. But we don't.

'And what will you do over there,' Mona asks, 'you know, for money?'

I tell her I've saved up a bit of cash from some office job I did a while back, that I don't spend much and that I can always teach English if I need to. I'm not really worried, mainly because I haven't thought about it, which is mostly because that would spoil the carefree nature of the endeavour. I say that I can easily take a flight home if the situation becomes difficult or I can't find work. I tell

DISTANT HILLS

her a few anecdotes about people I have met who live week by week, sleeping on beaches between hostel jobs, a tent and some sandwiches tucked between a few trees. Creeping back into civilisation at sun-up, hair in disarray, mischievous grins on their liberated cheeks. Healthy. Beaming with the secret knowledge of having lived in some better world where you still hear twigs snap on forest floors in the night, because that matters; and where there is no seven-second rule if you drop your focaccia on the ground, because that doesn't. A world where your eyes dart from side to side before you pull your bag out of the hedgerow. Where you have dirt on your hands and that's alright. I tell her about the time I was playing with a dung beetle at a desert resort in Morocco. Letting it onto and into my hand, repeating the motion. Its light leggy touch. About how the large group of Italian tourists with their flowery garlands were staring at me as if I should be reprimanded. Playing with an insect.

'You choose your own baseline,' I say, 'and sometimes you forget when you are near people who don't think the same things are okay as you think are okay. You know? And I like that, I like how we change. How you can contrive a thing at first, but eventually there's no escaping it, it's become yours. Turns out I play with beetles, it's not something I think about.'

'So, you're going to play with beetles over there?' says Dean.

And so it went for several hours. I knew I shouldn't have come. I'll answer a question if they ask it, and one will lead to a million more. Trapped in a topic. I'd change it, but what to? Why can't they pull us out of this? I didn't want to be leader but they hemmed me in, forcing me to sit in a box with my ego, and rattling it. I've drunk too much wine to be quiet and too much wine to listen to four people's conversation drift away from anything I know or care about. I've drank too much wine to go home; it would be a waste of a hangover. I need one-on-one conversation—fifty-fifty. I need to concentrate. I'm filling the spaces with more and more aspects to an answer, saying anything to stop the pauses creeping in. Pauses where I look to see what they think of me, and they look blankly back. Ram those gaps full of sentences, full of the movements of my face and arms. Keep them guessing, on the lookout for new information. They read me when I deflate between words. In the awkward smiles, and the need. All saggy before I start ploughing on again. I want to be equal. For that you need just one other person, head to head. One audience member, one performer. It's the only way.

I text a Lithuanian guy I went on a few dates with earlier in the year and he's around and suddenly we're in town and the bar's too dark and we're leaning in to one another when we don't really need to. He tells me how bored he is of everything and how we should do more, have more of an impact. And I'm with him, I get it. I tell him how hitchhiking is really cathartic because even when you have been sitting for hours, waiting for hours, you are still making progress, it still feels productive.

'Right, like cycling,' he says. 'You're going, you're moving somewhere, and it doesn't matter how slowly because it is only you. There's no waiting, no reliance on anyone else. And you're wet and you're sweaty but that's part of it too, that's the world all over you.'

'Up in your armpits!'

'There's no escape.'

'The greasy world!'

DISTANT HILLS

He smiles like a rascal, like a fifteen-year-old boy who has stolen a pig from a neighbourhood farm and now isn't quite sure what to do with it. Dimples. He taught me how to ride no-hands. Wheeling through the park I forgot the city was still close enough to look at me. I still do. When my back's straight and my thighs solid, I pretend I'm chewing gum and forget my few grey hairs and I actually start to swagger. Shoulders out and splayed like all I really want is a BMX and whatever the latest games console is for Christmas. Whenever I see women in their sixties or more riding down the dual carriageway I wonder what they might be imagining. I like it when it rains and we all smile at each other from beneath our hard helmets.

The Lithuanian has bought me another beer. A thick brown bottle. It feels good, sturdy. The sound of the first glug and the cold taste hitting the tongue; hold it before it becomes ordinary. Three swigs in and we've forgotten to notice. We are really laughing now. Simple, fifty-fifty. Me then him. You can pause in front of one person. You can falter in front of one person. It is okay when one person looks at you, when there are no adjacent elbows they might be nudging. No allies.

I look around the bar, long and labyrinthian, corners coming out of chairs coming out of tables. The edges of each possible viewpoint swaying into vignette. I smile at the bar man, younger than me; at the girl leaning nearby with the asymmetric hair line, blackened and half-waxed into lazy stalactites. I look into the background, hoping for a little extraordinary. The Lithuanian is telling me a story. There must be something in this bar I don't know. A decade passes. There's a hill, he says, in Lithuania, that looks like holy crosses have been poured out all over it. Like lava, he says, they come streaming out at you. Like, you don't see it getting any bigger but each time you go back there are more. Small paths have been hacked through, one person deep and one person wide. Eye-deep in crosses. Marys jumping out at you, waving, from the wooden right-angled bramble. 'You should go,' he says. 'We should go.'

I'm nodding and showing the right amount of surprise, which tends to come naturally after a few drinks. The sincerity, so hard to get right in the daytime, with new people, when I might be faking it. I'm perfect for a few minutes, a luminous fish darting about in cloudy water. Each motion creating bubbles, every shape rounded and smooth.

'I love this song,' he says. 'Dance with me, come on.'

And we're up. My pulled arm towing the rest of me. Loose body, sucker for momentum. Spinning makes the music louder and the room is both darker and brighter and I'm laughing and hating it but so glad to be mobile. Fast like a willow in the breeze. Cheeks ache and go red. Convince me to do this. Embarrassment and happiness and a certain percentage of alcohol. I could fall from the highest building, from a hot air balloon at the edge of the atmosphere. My stomach is the greatest thing.

I remember a time in the spring when I was at his house. He said he would put his favourite film on and he did. I was so bored. One-point-five hours until we could get on with it, conversation and dynamics and all the other things. So much of life is this stuff you've got to sit through until it gets interesting. If I was smarter I could have been working out algorithms in that time, solving real-life problems. Efficacy is key. I was so bored I determined never to see him again but I did because it was easy and not unpleasant. We didn't watch any more films together though and I didn't spend any more long evenings going through teenage photo albums in his house to help prompt the conversation. It was strictly social. Strictly bars and frivolity until we'd reached the right level of attracted. A couple of months like that before he went off to Wisconsin and I went to wherever I've just got back from and now here we are and now this is once again the same old thing.

We're whirling around, my radius against his, my comfort zone resting firmly on the back of my vacated chair; it's looking at me but I'm pretending not to notice. Eyes closed and at the ready. Arms linked into a figure eight. We are the most annoying people in this room. There isn't even a dance floor. Hips and thighs colliding tit-for-tat with humans and furniture. Foot wrapped round the leg of a chair, I'm down then up and I've never laughed so hard. He's kissing me and that's fine. I'll be able to sit down again in a moment.

I wake up in the Lithuanian's flat, about four or five in the morning, not quite light yet but the opacity is turning down. I go to the bathroom for water, creaking past the man's low rumbling body. Everything looks the same as I remember, more or less. The Japanese girl appears to have moved out but, as with all of them, her blu-tacked newspaper cuttings and postcards remain. An array of toiletry bottles that will never be used up. Unowned hairs and conglomerations of yellowish half-liquid dirt converging in circles along the bath and sink.

My eyes are older than some years ago; there is no way that is not the case. Imperceptible in the first instance, perhaps, but then inescapably and detrimentally obvious forever. I am older than I used to be. Parts of my body are undeniably complete. I stare into the mirror until my face goes missing, replaced by a blurred grey-black sphere from the left eye to the right ear, with cream-coloured penumbra and pink outline—like I've been censored. I think about Zlat in Croatia, and Kathy. I think about how it is good that I came here, that I let this happen. Because who knows what's been going on in Croatia. We didn't agree to anything. Only that I would come and he wanted me there and I wanted to leave.

I'd flown back to visit him from somewhere in Austria after steadfastly hitchhiking away, loyal to being alone for a while, to being scared of something. That lasted about a fortnight, until I realised I was just getting drunk near beautiful buildings in Vienna and waking up with yesterday's clothes on, complimentary hostel pillow beneath my knees. I messaged him and said, *What if I came back?*

He said *Come*, then he said *Stay*, then he said *Come back please*.

I slither back into the Lithuanian's bed, wrapping bits of me around his corresponding legwork. He doesn't stir. I know I've got to get out of here before he suggests watching films in bed all morning tomorrow. My nose drifts between his warm hairs and I wonder when/if next we will meet.

II.

I'M ON A hill, wind blowing through my hair and eddying round my knees. I am breathing in and it won't stop. The biggest breath I have ever taken, long and purposeful. Breathing in corners of the world, actual essences rising up toward my nostrils and becoming a part of me. I stretch out my arms through as much air as they can manage, becoming as wide as I can be. I roll a few little Croatian words along my tongue, subtle differences between consonants, pressing the tongue to the back of my teeth then hanging back slightly, not quite touching, bombing the air out through this new gap—relishing the mouthfeel. I stretch out into the space above this hill, the sea wet and small below me. My consonants sound like a steady, pushing ocean. I'm a sail, a great sail. All wind and aspiration. Croatia.

The sun hits me. Burning lasers. My skin builds a quick, red-hot fence around my body, which the sun rams into again and again. The day slouches but I stand tall and erect, an anvil on a tuft of grass, bellowing grandiose syllables into the bright night air.

Kathy sent me a *missing you* email with an attachment photograph of her and her happy little children waving, faces crushing each other's different-sized faces into an undersized frame. That was this morning. It's only been seventy-two hours, so it seems like a bit of an exaggeration. Probably just caught up in the action. Someone takes a plane somewhere and people think it's an event of some kind. Still, I appreciate the sentiment. I think about if she could see me now, with this hill under my jurisdiction, my pale skirts flapping. Not quite the pathetic loser I used to be, oh no, not me. No longer coiled up inside an off-grey and once-lavender sleeping bag on somebody else's living-room floor. A sleeping bag I've owned for approximately a third of my existence: one of those objects you travel through life with. Buy one get one free. I remember the day, I remember the shop. I wonder where its partner is. Twisting its way around an old friend's squirming body as she dreams?

No longer unrolling myself in the morning, kick-swimming my legs until the bag inches its way far enough down toward my knees. No. Now I am in Croatia and the boy owns his own apartment and he's made a space for me. He has cleared me a shelf or two in the bedroom, a shelf or three in the kitchen. He brought out a cream-and-green striped mug with thick sides and said *this one can be yours.* He said *you can use the other ones too, of course, but this one is especially yours.* I rolled it between my hands and rubbed the sides and pressed the bottom with my thumb. I put it on my shelf, in the middle where the Croatian food would go once I had bought it. I put one of Zlat's hands in the space where the mug had been and I rubbed the sides and pressed the bottom with my thumb. I asked if we could go to buy onions because my mug was lonely and he put another mug next to it, with a picture of three robins on it, one singing, and his phone and his keys. Then he closed the door to the cupboard, put one of his fingers vertically across his two lips and comedy-tiptoed away. High knees, like walking on the moon.

The dog took a shit on the living-room floor this morning. Half past twelve I saw it, right in the centre. I had been for a walk to the shop to buy Croatian food, had walked along some roads which were higher than some of the other roads, had looked down. The dog is called To Be, Tobey. It looks at me; acute head, asymmetrical eyes. I do not clean up the shit, I ignore it. I make sure to leave the house again and to remain left until after Zlat comes home. He'll see it, he'll clean it. He will think I spent the day outside, or the afternoon, that the poo arrived after I departed, that I did not know. I do not like this dog. I don't like the way it sleeps at the end of this bed that I share now. Its paws, hooks, claws, twitching. It pooed because it hates me, too. A stupid needy thing with no real language. All charm and organs. I never wanted a dog, did not realise I would have one. It wasn't something I considered. Or a new Croatian mother. She feeds me cakes and looks down at my belly.

I am twenty-eight years old and I have learnt the word for stupid and the word for humidity. I understand how to conjugate some of the verbs. Zlat is thirty, and with a robust arm behind my neck, a shoulder pit and hand on top of each of my shoulders, he tells me he thinks he is too old to change. That he is finished formulating his opinions. I take this phrase and put it in one of the parts of my brain that remembers things which might one day come in useful when imparting knowledge or compiling wisdom. I do not think I will be finished at thirty or fifty or sixty, or even when I am lying in a bed, the pillows of which somebody else has plumped for me, familiar pains circulating their familiar territories, a neck full of pills I've hastily swallowed so I can finally finish everything. I do not think I will be finished even then, even when I am done for.

I remember when Kathy was pregnant the first time and I touched her bulbous stomach. Hard like my thighs after I cycled to Antwerp and couldn't walk down the stairs properly one evening at the end. Hard like the arms of the dying. Skin shouldn't feel like that; it should have a little leeway. *I'm just popping to the shop*, Kathy would say, while I sleeping-bagged the hours away on her plush shag carpet, and all I could see until she came back were echoes of her fertile body exploding. All over the double yellow lines, all over the single white lines—parked cars, wing mirrors, cyclists. Hard like a wall. Built like a brick shithouse. Being born.

Zlat tells me to put a dress on and we're going out. *Not to the boat*, he says, *somewhere else*. All his friends, the ones that come out regularly, are male apart from the one female with very short hair, and they all have names of one syllable and four letters, apart from Aleksandar. Aleksandar carries a Freddie Mercury doll in his pocket and waves it in the air when the songs come on. Aleksandar says he wants to be a prince and marry a queen who rides a horse. He mime-gallops up to women at bars and asks them questions about peasantry, serfdom, kingdoms. He fake-unmounts and reallife-curtsies, rolling his hand as he lowers, like his *R*s. He tells me that when this works, him and Freddie will have found a home at last, and that he's not too worried about how long it might take because

DISTANT HILLS

his horse has another twenty years or so of life in her yet. He winks at me as he fake-pats its hide. His arm is around me and we sway a bit like dancing. We *are* the champions, we are, I know it.

There's a section of road where some artists have painted a pedestrian crossing in an alleyway that leads from one wall to another. It's my favourite way to walk home and I say so and we do it loudly. Zlat's telling me how glad he is I came; that he was counting down the days, holding his trousers together. That it's his birthday next week and I'm here and he can't believe this is a thing that is actually happening. I tell him I love him and that I am so excited, because that's the thing to say next and maybe I do.

We met on a fold-out sofa bed three months ago in a room with no dog in it. When Zlat was twenty-nine and hadn't finished forming his opinions yet. He took his clothes off and I took my clothes off because sometimes that is the best way to learn about somebody. His belly felt hard and round as it jutted into mine, but then you get used to it, the shapes of other people's bodies. My arms don't fit around him; each hug a challenge. I can just keep on going, stretching my arms out wide into the air. If Kathy or any of them could see me now, holding on to all this. Galloping with this horse.

I spend the afternoons reading, moving objects around, walking, not walking. I'm playing house in a foreign land. I'm out there in the world buying groceries. My shelves are full. I've got a life here now, something definitive to mess about with. I could fit the summary on a postcard, send it home, write a blog post. We could make Christmas cards with pictures of me and Zlat and that fucking dog on, wearing red felt hats with white fur trim and grinning. All fuzzy off the šljivovica, Zlat in the middle.

We have gone to Italy for the weekend, just the tip of it, just to be somewhere. We drove through the ice-cream hills and up out of the city, past the little broken bits of history that now sprout weeds. We sit on wicker chairs in disintegrating plazas drinking small, strong coffees and saying *this is the life, oh it is, isn't it.* Or, at least, I'm trying to but Zlat keeps correcting my word endings. Passing Italian people glance at us and think *look at those two Croatians, with their small, strong Italian coffees, thinking this is the life.* I lean back in the chair and Zlat is on the phone to someone. I am thinner than before and a little more tanned. I am tired and I lack routine. I wonder what I look like from a pair of Italian eyes, with Zlat; how one's company changes the way we are seen. Zlat is staring right at me. I ask him who he was talking to and he says it was one of his fuck buddies. There is a brief pause before Italy crumbles. Zlat's left cheek moves up slightly, his eyes focus. He tells me not to worry, he explained to her that I had arrived and she couldn't come over anymore. Right. Eyes thick on the way to tsunami. Coffee to the mouth and back. Keep those arms working. Flex.

In the hotel room Zlat tells me I look beautiful when I'm jealous. He wanted to see.

By the time I am thirty-five I would like a faux-fur trailing coat, a wheely suitcase, and a fold-away umbrella. To be more successful at being an adult woman these are the things I will need. Also, obviously, a good man by my side, regular ovulation, a rich and rewarding career, girlfriends, travel. I haven't found a job yet but I'm not spending much money. Food, coffee. Everywhere I go I walk to, up and down the Croatian hills. Once a week I meet Zlat's friend Dasha in a cafe on the harbour to eat fish and share a decanted bottle of wine with and look out at the sea. She has a faux-fur collar because autumn has started and she is doing better than me at adapting to the passage of the years. The first few weeks she was without one; all strappy-sleeved and broad plateau of shoulders, but then she brought the faux-fur with her and I was like, yes, I'll keep this one, she's an inspiration. Most of Zlat's female friends stay at home with their cute Croatian offspring while the men come out and drink and dance and throw up a bit and wipe their mouths before they teeter off home again.

Not Dasha. Perfectly independent and elegant Dasha. We stare at each other and then at the ocean, sharing long, knowing silences during which we contemplate our different but not so very different lives. Dasha is thirty-eight and her hair curls around her face like a period drama. Painted fingernails and cigarette after cigarette with lipstick-stained ends. The sunset suits her. Profile, silhouette, perimeter, everything. She was made to have the sun shine just off to the side and slightly behind her. Born to have a background. I get close enough to emulate her gestures. Tiny hand movements under the table where she cannot see. I lift her cigarette to my knee. Purse my lips imperceptibly, pretending to smoke it. Red wine and the ocean. A milkshake, yogurt-like, cream. I want to be like her. She wears lace at the ends of her sleeves.

She tells me Zlat is one of her best friends but that she would never date him. Tells me he doesn't really like women, if I know what she means. I tell her I broke up with someone a month before I met him, in Armenia, and I didn't really care after that what happened to me. She calls me a free-spirit. I tell her I love her and do an over-emphasised Japanese-style bow, straight back, arms out. I think I might mean it. I pretend my hat has fallen off and excuse myself as I pretend to pick it up again. We look at the almost empty wine decanter and she shakes it and looks a bit coy and afraid so I raise my eyebrows and move their eyeballs left to right in quick refrain. She fake-suppresses a gigantic laugh then bursts and nods her head like we've just correctly answered a tricky question and sticks the front of her red-wine tongue between her rows of lipstick teeth and squeals. She asks me to tell her about the trains and buses I took from Armenia to get here as the wine starts from the beginning again. She half-closes her eyes and nods away as I detail the smells, the people, the carriage décors. She grabs my wrist and pulls. We run towards what remains of the sun, to the water. I love it when it goes dark on us, when it all ends but we keep on going in. Lace in the water. Bags and faux-fur on the sand. It's the red wine that keeps the summer from leaving us. I am mesmerised by this world that holds me. By this woman I do not know who knows this man I should know better. We float out to the nearest boat moored, touch it, bob about a bit and float back again.

I try to tell her I have never seen phosphorescence and that I would like to, except I can't say it and she can't say it, neither in English nor in Croatian. We try with our mouths full of sea water to see if it helps any but it doesn't. We spit our way out of the water to where Zlat stands, arms folded, one eyebrow cocked at us girls, holding a beer.

'Come on,' he says, 'the guys are waiting, there's a gig at Akademia. Band from Zagreb. Accordions. You want some dry clothes?'

DISTANT HILLS

I nod and Dasha nods and asks to be dropped off at home. She leaves to have a bubble bath and continue being elegant while I get so drunk I can't remember anything apart from holding Aleksandar's hand in the fog of it all on the dance floor and yelling Croatian tongue twisters into a barman's ear. I wake up with the top half of my clothes still on and an unwelcome dog beneath my knees. Zlat's gone to work and I don't walk the dog or go to the shop or eat anything or drink enough fluid or look for a job. I spend an hour looking at winter coats online. I spend another hour looking at pictures of women inside winter coats online. I lose a bit of time just staring at the shape of the mouse and at the keyboard and trying to remember how to spell a few Croatian things. I look at a map of Croatia and Serbia and Bosnia and the rest, and think about that for a while. I try to read a few of the place names with word roots like *mushroom* and *egg*. I remember a truck driver in Bosnia who couldn't read the Cyrillic alphabet. He didn't know what any of the signs said that he drove past, didn't want to. Just remembered the way. I go to the toilet, long, hot and powerful, and check the colour. Dark yellow. I get a glass of water and think about kicking the dog.

I ring Aleksandar but he does not answer. I ring the girl with short hair but she does not answer. I shout at the dog but it does not answer. I take it for a walk. People are looking at me as if this is my dog. As if I am a Croatian and both I and the dog belong here, together. As if this is my dog and this is the way I walk it. But this is not my dog. I don't even like this dog. I want to say horrible things in English to the dog and then ignore it forever. I want to treat it very badly, knowing that it can't tell anyone. I want Zlat to be in love with me and then when he's at work I want to be the worst person in the world to this animal until it sorts its head out and runs away. Then I want to comfort Zlat and understand what he's going through while he rests his big sad skull on my knee. I tug the dog's lead a little forcefully but nothing more.

Zlat doesn't come home from work so I don't feed the dog. When he does come home I will tell him I fed it and then the dog will lose. I check my bank account and I email Kathy. Guilt keeps nudging me so I throw the dog a scrap of dark rye bread I can't be bothered to continue eating. Low light, automatic brightness on the computer screen. A text message from the Lithuanian on my phone saying he's going to Slovenia in a couple of weeks and do I want to meet? I think I'm actually rocking slightly. Kathy is online and I think about telling her how hungover I am and the fact that Zlat's not home and that I miss her and my head hurts and I might be hungry. I say *Hey*. Five or so minutes later she says *Hey* back and tells me they've bought a new car and they are going to the coast for the weekend. That hopefully they will see puffins. She asks if I remember when we used to watch wildlife documentaries together. Says she was watching some of them with some of the children the other night and she thought about me. How we used to copy the movements, leaping and wading through the reeds and the corals that were really ornaments and ironing boards and bits of Christmas trees. That's nice. That's enough.

I try not to think too much about what Zlat is doing because he talks in Croatian on the phone a lot to a woman's voice and before I arrived he told me he expects to have sex at least twice a day, and

I've counted and we're not quite on target. Before I arrived, during the Lithuanian era, he told me he'd had sex with three women between when we saw each other last and when we saw each other next because he couldn't stop thinking about me. I told him it was fine and I liked that he had told me and it actually made me feel a bit sexy. I told him this while we were sitting on a wall sharing a bottle of beer and pointing at a few of the stars we could see. But now I don't think I feel at all sexy. I think I mostly feel like stabbing the dog and telling it to fuck off when it comes near me. I try to write a few emails to Kathy, with punctuation and capitals and line breaks, but I delete them all and instead press down on the letter *E*, watching how the pattern repeats.

I text Aleksandar. He tells me I can meet him and Freddie down near the boat bar if I want, so I feed the dog and then I go. Freddie is sat on a bench outside the bar with a little note attached to him that says 'Aleksandar bar. Has go get drinks.' I fold the scrap of paper into a quick little aeroplane, lay it on Freddie's lap, pointing bar-ward, and follow Aleksandar in. He trots over on his horse, two bottles in hand, and tugs the reins.

'Was she the one?' I ask.

'Unfortunately, no this time. She not understand how treat horse. She know not how prince needs.'

I grab the beer and smile.

We walk along the deck of the boat; chairs here and there, people who look too young to be kissing, kissing. A small bat flickers in and out of my attention. *I don't know how long I'll be here, Aleksandar*, I say, except I don't because he's my boyfriend's friend and we're not supposed to confide in each other. All we are allowed to do is get drunk and dance in groups and occasionally hold hands in the dark. Which we do; me, him and Mercury; until it's time to not remember going home again and I wake up and Zlat still isn't there.

Zlat says we're moving in with his mother because he wants to rent out his apartment. She really likes me, he says. I'll pick up the language much quicker there. It's forty minutes out of the centre by bus, and the buses stop around 1 a.m. There's one bus an hour at night, uphill, and taxis are hard to come by. I tell Zlat I'm not sure but we sit for hours on the very same couch we first got reckless on, talking about all the trips we could take with the extra money, the people we might meet and the things we might say to each other. Rain-soaked cheeks, a brutal wind lashing against our waterproof jackets, clammy palms in each other's clammy palms: invincible. I think about how nothing matters other than the present moment and the possibility of anything being possible. How it's probably good practice for my personality to not be jealous of things. To not be paranoid. We sit up all night, blankets wrapped in arms wrapped up in blankets. Watching the Croatian news. Learning what so many of the words are. Zlat says the syllables again and again. I try to repeat them, spit flying everywhere. The twinkles of our eyes synchronise. His sweat is warm against my own. He closes the door and we are dogless together.

I love being in Croatia. The sun's rays heating up my skull like a microwave. I bask as I walk around, closing my eyes, peeking out through a half-open lid at the thought of traffic. I haven't found a job yet. Money has a way of lasting. There is nothing I really want and nothing I really need. It is enough that my feet experience the

DISTANT HILLS

texture of tarmac or sand through the soles of my shoes. Sometimes I get my feet bare and touch the sea and sand with them and, sand stuck on and under and around the nails, pop them in the socks again; feel it grate. Cloth on my shoulders, a waistband. When it is hot everything has a way of touching you. The concrete looks like Spanish resorts as you get closer to the shore. Some days I just sit there, reliving things I've lived once already, and eating ice cream.

I throw the pan to the ground by its handle. Two-dimensional flying egg saucers hit the kitchen floor and dissipate. Yolks drooling into the tongue of that dog, always alert and waiting. Tears are pouring down my bronzer-than-usual face and most of my muscles are quivering. Tense then not. I try to scream, but a silencer or widget is stuck in my throat. The only noise I am able to make is a kind of glottal air-wheeze. Zlat's looking at me like he's watching a TV show about an auction; vaguely interested but he doesn't have the reference points to understand what any of the prices or objects mean. I see his eyes at mine, considering but also wanting to leave. He fingers the lock of the door and mutters something I won't understand. I take my panting a little closer to his exit. Loud and wet I drop it on the floor. My back against the pale blue metal door. Dragged my legs through egg juice to get here. Zlat's still got his index finger and thumb on the lock. On the handle, turning. There is no reaction from him, so I do it for the both of us, to help us make some progress. I try to keep it to a maximum. I can't believe there is nothing inside him that can make me stop. All he needs to do is press a switch or say a word; make an effort. But nothing. I want to destroy everything I can just to see him act.

Nothing. I am scrunched up. A tightness. Like a flung paper bag if that bag were cursing in English and wailing. He forces the door and it opens towards him and into me. My origami-rose shaped body is shimmied along the linoleum, screaming.

I don't feed the dog. I don't look at it. I don't take it for a walk. Except I can see it in my peripheral vision with its stupid head cocked, trusting me. I get back in Zlat's bed and pull the covers around everything except my nose and eyes and a small part of the top of my head, where the parting is or would be if my hair wasn't sticking out all ways, mangled with grease and fear. My eyes are red and fat like the skin that lives under the first few layers of unbitten fingertip; like uncooked salmon. There's a great calm, a reassurance at the point when you realise you can't cry any longer; the body relaxes, slows, it feels like new life after having recovered from a terrible fever. Like you've just been told everything will be okay and rocked to sleep by a human twice your size. Some of the nicest sleeps come after crying, when the covers billow in a soothing breeze. The opposite of that shape in your throat that does all the scratching.

I sleep for a while, wrapped up like my own dear treasure, then I check my eyes are okay to go out into the world again and walk the dog and pretend to love it. Some ships are out on the sea. Masts signalling to me, making me look up. Seagulls feeling free. I let the dog off the lead but it follows me home anyway, sniffing the length of the other side of the street. The girl with the short hair tries to phone me. I don't answer. I get back into my bed of curl and text Aleksandar. He tells me the crusaders are besieging Zagreb tonight but he'll see me soon. Minutes stretch out like old threads we try to

DISTANT HILLS

find the ends of but the fabric keeps on coming. I can't even look. The sun is simply stuck there. That dog the only thing left with any life inside. I pull my laptop to me and sit with it, flicking from tab to tab. There is nothing. None of the ticks I need are green.

III.

THE TRAIN PULLS into central Ljubljana in just under three hours. I've had the carriage to myself for the last couple of stations, watching the bales of hay and cart-tugging raspberry sellers sliding by. Small bodies of water, the backs of houses, occasional cars. My eyeballs flutter from one thing to the next. I have not read more than a page of the book I have been holding since long before the useless border. Thoughts about other train journeys I have made, the differences between then and now, how even mini-disc players have their own kind of nostalgia. The girl with the other half of the pair of sleeping bags currently lives in Canada. In Armenia I was walked away from as a truck pulled up to take us at the side of an unkempt road. He walked away and I watched the way he walked as he receded. Looked up at the driver who was looking down at me and shook my head. The driver gestured to the passenger seat a few more times, open-handed and eyebrows high so I knew he was safe, serious. But no. I turned back to the road to where the way the man I knew walked used to be; the cars all trying to stop for me now I was solo. A cloud of dust. You do get to where you are going eventually; it's almost impossible not to. One train connects with another. She moved to Canada three years ago last summer and I kept saying I would visit her but I never did.

I guess she doesn't have the sleeping bag anymore; it's usually me that holds on to things. We matched like twins. T-shirts, trousers, the way we dreamed. Pretending to be annoyed with each other but secretly we liked it, showing off in front of strangers, occasionally letting a third one join in. Competing in the way that whenever one pulled away they eventually stopped and waited for the other to catch up again. Left for love, stayed for work, or vice versa. Hardly important. I just left because everyone else was leaving and I didn't want to be the last one at the party, too exhausted to move, wishing someone would come and turn the music down. I don't remember the last time we had a verbal conversation. Maybe we're shy now; it happens.

He happened. Said I was ruining the whole trip, that everything was better without me. Flinched when I tried to put my body slightly closer to his body. I should have planned it better, the grand finale; could have been in Europe. Who fights in Armenia? Russia was right next door and even they didn't muscle back in. Beautiful place though, from what I could see through the tears. Can't really remember how I got out of there—a world shrunk to my very next move. Being scared will do that, make you a tunnel to run to the end of. You have a quick look around, weigh up your options and scurry back down. Until you are safely in a sleeper carriage, wheels clattering on, and you have a few days to decipher the name of the city at the end of your ticket. I crocheted a scarf to remember the length of the journey by, to say, *yeah, this is what happened, this is what I did.* It wasn't very good in the end so I threw it away, saying, *yeah, this is what I think about what I did and about the things that happened.* That way I still had something tangible in my memory to help me explain.

The train pulls into central Ljubljana, my eyes reconnect with the present day. Legs and elbows race for the corridor, bodies like tessellating *S*s all fighting for their little piece of aisle space. Between the fold-down side-facing chairs, smoking waste places, and goldbrass sliding-door handles, I organise my centre of gravity in the maze of limbs, lock my feet in a steady position, and brace myself for the alighting wave.

Ljubljana. Castles like milky candles, melting and dirty. Dragons and luminescent cobbles dotted about all over. The kind of city where you want to see magic tricks and rub everything. I saw a fairy in the park, I'm sure of it. Me and the Lithuanian are in a cave that sells beer, knees under and elbows on a rickety old table-like structure in a corner, and he's asking me how big it was, was anyone else with me, did I document it, that sort of thing. I'm laughing and trying to pretend I don't know where I'm sleeping tonight, except he's already let slip he's got a double room and used the word *us* at least nine times during the last two beers. He's brought his dimples out with him and they look good in this country, he looks good here. I imagine him turned into marble, smog under his eyelids and melting slowly over millennia. Slovenia suits him.

I tell him I like his hair and he says he likes mine too and a little bit of my brain bashes against itself in a bid to make all this somehow more interesting. I could have checked in to a hostel, in a dif-

DISTANT HILLS

ferent city, or gone back to the country where I started and just ridden it out, but it's all so predictable. People talking English to each other and making lists of the places they have been. He's telling me a story about a zoo for birds, which might be in Belgrade, where they've got a duck with a teal head, a pigeon, a chicken (scrawny old thing), some sparrows. He thinks it's all very funny and now his phone's out, he's flicking through his pictures, there was also an ostrich. I look at a picture on his phone that is mostly a photograph of the larger portion of the Lithuanian's face but also a little bit a photograph of an ostrich. I tell him I like what he's done with the Golden Ratio there and he says *what?* and I wave my hand and head about while I look down slightly and say *never mind*.

He wants to go dancing but I want to be drunk and walk around in the outside. I win because I'm buying, so I buy four to win faster and then there's little he can do to oppose.

I love it when there's purple in the air. Grey and blue and purple, that's how I want the sky. Soapy and vague. Fog mixed with velvet and flickers of ice. We step-step on the cobbles, every perfect one. Shining from all the many times they've been walked over—carriages with horses, years of trade. Lights pounding out of all the shops selling fridge magnets, brightly coloured trousers with too-low crotches, and hats with long tassels that dangle past the ears. We look in some of the shops and touch a few of the things. A Slovenian lady nods at us from her corner where she sits under lamplight. Doing something delicate with a needle. Glasses down the end of her nose. Lonely nights. Tourists buying nothing, saying nothing, understanding nothing. I buy a fridge magnet because I want her to know that she could be my mother too, and we could all be happy.

'Come on!' I scream. 'There's no time to lose! Let's find the biggest hill we can and run up it. Yes, you bring sandwiches. Twenty minutes, back here. I shower, you shower. You grab food, I grab food. Perfect co-ordination. A simple life where everything works first time.'

I exit the bathroom with a hotel-white, 500GSM towel tucked around the upside of my torso, swing a quick 180, hooking the Lithuanian's crooked elbow through my own crooked elbow, and in he jives serenading his pre-packaged sandwich toward the steam.

'This hill isn't very big.'

'No.'

'It looked bigger from the bottom.'

'Yeah.'

'My legs don't even hurt. I mean, I'm pressing right down into the muscle and I can't feel a thing.'

'Maybe tomorrow. Sometimes you think you've got away with it and then, bam, you really feel that next-morning hobble to the bathroom.'

'Hmm, hopefully. Let's not stretch, and see if we can make it happen.'

I start to do a stretch but the Lithuanian bats my ankle out of my hand, tells me I'm spoiling it. I spend most of the afternoon pretending to break out into a lunge or that hamstring exercise every time he pretends to not be looking. He makes me take him to where I think I saw the fairy. We sit on swings there, a small half-neglected park behind the unwanted sides of a couple of Soviet-style apartment buildings. We don't see the fairy because we are trying too hard, and there are too many of us witness in the day's blaze.

He doesn't believe me but I don't care because it doesn't affect the fact of my once having believed in it. Like that time I saw an alien crawling out of the communal bin at the end of a row of terraced houses on a street I once lived on. It only lasted for a second probably but I learnt a lot about myself, and aliens, in that short time: who I would tell first, how much I can keep my cool in adverse situations. Turned out to be a bin bag flapping about in the pre-dawn breeze, but, still, it happened, we still looked at each other. I remember it froze when it clocked me, stopped scavenging, just hung there. Neither of us knew what to do, so I rubbed my eyes and blinked and focused and that turned out to have been the correct thing. Shame though. I really thought I was on to something.

The Lithuanian is looking at me like we are in this together, but I don't think we are. In fact, I'm very much certain we're not. I go along with it anyway, so as not to rock any boats today: he's on holiday. I tell him I'd quite like to go back to the hotel room, send a few emails. If that's a thing, if that's okay, me in the room. I don't want to assume anything. He extends his arm round the back of my skull, hooks his elbow pit into my neck side, and moves the top half of me to the right, spine like a hurried tent peg. Lithuanian lips on my forehead grooves. Body position stretching out one of my two sides. I wriggle out and hop off the swing, wide-lunge across the grass, hands on my hips like I mean it. He hamstring-chases me until three or four excited children, faces concurrently in all directions, nearly collide with us and we straighten up before the inevitable adults see our behaviour. Fake-whistling and making our hairs neat.

Kathy has sent me an email. Laptop at the feet end of the hotel-room bed, elbows stiff and bony. My fingers wiggling around—antennae. Knees face down, if they had any. Feet oscillating to no particular rhythm at the pillow end of the air. This is the position I associate most with being a teenager. This is how I thought it would be for years and years. Except it wasn't exactly a computer then, more of a lever-arch ring binder or a magazine telling you where your boobs are. The devices changed but the position stayed the same. Even when I was nineteen, twenty, twenty-one. Never really thought beyond lying on a bed like this, flinging myself into position, elbows down, head up, beginning to exist. Free but not too free; still getting my dinner cooked and having a guaranteed place to sleep. *What's going on?* says the email. *I've seen a couple of photos of you in Slovakia or somewhere! Why aren't you in Croatia? Is that that guy? He looks familiar. That's not the Croatian, is it? Have I seen him before? What's going on?*

I read the email three times, go to the toilet, read it again. Hit reply, hover, hit discard. There isn't really anything I want to say. Better to be mysterious rather than back-and-forthing with your own postcode from afar. She will find these little allusions to me floating around in the night sky; let her wonder. Better that way than my explanations. Better than trying to be in the same room when you're not. We couldn't grip the other's forearm if we were slowly tumbling down the stairs from here. No point answering her question just because she asked it. We're supposed to think about things. We're supposed to go away, far away, and then come back.

DISTANT HILLS

I never really thought beyond lying on a bed like that; obsessed about it for years, waiting to be thirteen. I leapt, sprung. Six years passed in the blink of a push-up, hoisting myself off before I threw myself down again. Then it was gone. The beds doubled and the patterns of the covers suddenly all had flowers on. I was supposed to have a reading corner, sit on a sensible chair in the half-light and cross, uncross my legs. Glancing delectably upwards when the visitors came and when they left. Sitting in coffee shops, taking my crossword puzzle out of one of my handbags, taking off my leather gloves and placing them one atop the other next to my saucer and receipt on the mahogany table. I want to wear shorts down to my knees and not wash my hair and to lie on my stomach reading the latest whatever on the concourse of a train station. Wheely suitcases and business shoes riding overhead, excusing themselves each time they knock the pages.

I close the laptop. My back hurts if I lie too long like that.

The Lithuanian says he's going to a nearby lake tomorrow in a rented car with a couple of people he met in the pre-packaged-sandwich shop this morning. There's a space in the car if I want to go along, but I've seen lakes before so I'll make other plans. We go out for dinner. Food for him and food for me. Cutting it up into manageable portions. Talking through the half-dissolved wine-soaked morsels that cling between our teeth. I should go to the lake, he says. Hell, if I don't have any plans, I should go with him to Hungary. We could rent bicycles and cycle all the way to the Belarusian border, and then cross it, he says. His eyes shiny and walked-all-over like the cobbles outside. 'I'm going north,' I say, 'it's non-debatable. We can go dancing after dinner if you want though?' Droplets of rain on the cobbles. Cluster bombs. A little silence. Knives on traditional Slovenian chopping boards.

There are three hours to wait until the next train northward. I am feeding disappointing crisps to pigeons on one of the platforms and trying not to look at anyone. When you are hungover it feels like they all know where you've been. I slipped out early, before the Lithuanian groaned himself awake again. Climbed out of bed, over his obstacle legs and hurdle chest. Tried not to disturb him. A note is easier than saying goodbye in real-time. Especially with heads like these. His arm came with me as I tried to walk away from the mattress: determined hand seeks ungrabbed wrist. I peeled it off finger by finger, tucked it back in. *Speak soon,* I wrote on a flattened sheet of toilet paper. *Email me.* I wedged a corner under his masculine deodorant bottle, called something like Engine or Untameable, between his peeling watch strap and a stray earplug that was not entirely clean. He grumbled, repositioned, muttered something vague.

At the station, my face in my hands, the odours of coconuts and stale lager compete. Zlat tries to call me. I don't answer due to the roaming charges and the pain I feel.

IV.

ELSE LOBS A snowball hard at my side. Harder than she meant to. It was a good shot. Ice-flakes melting down the inside of my ear. I shake it off, launch at her, and press her red raw cheeks down into the dirt. She kicks me away, spitting snow out of her face, and I'm on my back, rolling my eyes up to the streetlight stars. It's never dark in Amsterdam, merely underlit. I make footsteps in the snow, concentric circles going out or going in. Else links me and we take our shining cheeks along a canal periphery until we might be back where we started. The snowthing we built four weeks ago is still standing, helps me navigate. As do the fairy lights on the first floor of the apartment block on that corner I always forget is a corner near the old cinema. Canal does a sharp turn instead of the usual meander, takes me by surprise every time. It's on the crease of the pocket map I carry, so there is no way to remember until you get there and remember once again that you forgot. Else takes her glove off and looks at her hand trying to move its fingers to see how cold they are, and then puts the glove back on. She smiles and hugs herself, contracting every major muscle in her body; as if a great wind is coming and she is the only permanent structure. Snow falls and floats on our eyelashes, hats, and hair. A light dusting of flour. Finishing touches. I have been here for four months.

The apartment room is small, fourth floor. A stairway that narrows and creaks. Old wood, damp in the nostrils. I bend at the knees and breathe. Pause at the corners and look behind, down into the murky water. Look at where I've been. Ten steps, four steps, hands on warped banisters, fingers in the cleaves. Past the limbs of bicycles dangling by their chains. Real, solid frames. Titanium, steel. So much more than this banister that melts and fades. I drag my downward tending body to the layer I need and shake my boots off while I insert the key.

A kettle boils. Music is playing softly and drifting in at me through the door cracks. Across the threshold and up around the frame and hinges. Jaap knocks on my little seal, three tentative taps, the last a slightly longer pause away from the second than the second from the other one. I walk over from the bed, blanket pulled around to keep the draft out, cardigan zipped to the chin. *Thanks*, I say, taking the mug while I look at his forty-seven-year-old face, the way it's about to sink in. He nods an awkward nod, using the full top half of his body. Shoulders hunched, his neck apologising. Scared of females, of foreigners, of people younger and older than him. I like the way his feet shuffle along, sweeping the floor as he goes. Coaxing their filthy grey slippers along.

I like the way we don't talk to each other. Pottering in and out of the rooms. My body, his body. Windows from the top of the

DISTANT HILLS

ground to the bottom of the next ground highlighting everything we see. I like to sit on the bean bag, silently, and point my eyes out. Looking at it all and then down at my knees. Narrow buildings that resemble owls. Feeling the warmth of tea through ceramic. I can smell the clouds and the boats and the silt uprooted from canal beds, now swirling aimlessly around. Steam on the glass. My own heat. The difference between outside and in. The apartment room is small, I have a 75-litre backpack that doesn't quite contain everything I need.

Two short shelves and a single-doored wardrobe, no hangers. Clothes folded into squares or thereabouts and then layered by colour. I open the door, stoop. I go in. Try to wear the ones at the bottom of the pile too or you'll forget that you have them. Rotate, mix it up a bit. Point your head down and see if you think the combination looks okay from up here.

Me and Jaap, Jaap and me. He walks around my items and I around his. I met Else a week after I arrived, dropping my trainers on Netherlandian soil. She was working at the Irish bar to fund her dreams. Then she quit, so either her dreams don't need funding anymore or she no longer has any. I didn't ask. She got me my first shift. Jaap is in there most nights, slurping away on a watery Guinness. Foam on hairs on shivering lip. He leaned over, right over, the first time I served him. The way people do when it's loud and you're from somewhere they think might be exotic and they think you won't know how to click. Not quite patronising, but loud and simple: you're on their turf and this is how it is. He asked me what music I like to listen to, how long I'd been here, what did I think about this city, his.

A few Guinnesses and some volume of Belgian beer later, and

leaning over the bar towards Jaap and his friends, Anouk and Wim, I might have answered him. Some of the passing detail might have counted, might have made it through to the following morning. And as they cycled home, weaving in and out of the parked, unparked, and abandoned bicycles, bumping about on the cobbles, elasticated saddles and rears, they might have exchanged a phrase or two, a thought or two; *they do look like owls; their lyrics are very experimental; I do have a spare room.*

I stayed in the hostel for ten nights before Jaap raised my hand and let my hand drop firmly and said I could move in. The hostel smelt of weed trails and hovering fertility, so I was glad to be collecting my passport from behind the counter and handing back my rented sheets. I packed my things, which that morning still just about condensed themselves into the 75-litre backpack, while four electronic guys from London snored around me, dreaming their drum-and-bass scenarios and creaking the bunk-bed beams.

Sometimes I climb back to the flat to find Jaap sitting in silence in the gradual darkness, hot mug of liquid steaming up into his unlit facial scenes.

'Hi.' I click the lights.

'Hoi.' He squints.

I flick off my shoes, and they flick off their snow, onto the not quite real wooden panelling of the almost hallway. Two cold steps and I'm in my room, a silhouetted top-half human shape can be seen through the frosted interior window, as Jaap skulks past to the toilet for the third time that hour, embossed with glassy leaves. I slot my little door in place, leap onto the bed, and press my teenage stomach against the flowery sheets. Lower legs to-and-froing, remembering lever-arch ring binders with graffitied bats on the inside covers. Jaap clicks off the lights.

    I reach over and grab my laptop—metallic green. Slide my palms across its textured, gentle surface. The way the top half rotates open; a smooth and constant resistance against the tiny force of my right hand. Haven't logged on for days in order to make sure I have definitely made it here, in my lit-up room in this lit-up city in the middle of the day, in the middle of winter, in the middle of the filmset nights. I am trying to focus but all I seem to be able to think about is train journeys through the Caucasus, dogs looking on as cool metal doors slide into heaps of me, and how I never really got to know Freddie Mercury as much as I would have liked. I have three emails from Kathy and a .gif from Aleksandar. I open the .gif first because that's the easiest thing: a knight in armour slamming a battle axe into where the ground would be if someone had coded it in.

    Kathy is pregnant. The fourth time. I find a .gif of a large human with a queue of smaller humans trailing after it like baby ducks, and attach that to an email with a pitch for my name as potential middle-name candidate. She'd be worried if I didn't. I'd be surprised if she did. I don't know what else to write. I tell her about the Irish bar, about Else and how we cycle around the country when the wind allows, between the canals, through the geometric orchards. I tell her how flat and serene the planet is from this angle. Although I phrase it differently, something along the lines of *it's really nice here, I like it, you should come visit*, but she won't, can't; could, doesn't realise how easy it is.

    I open the .gif of the knight again. Watch it slam that axe a couple of hundred times while my brain drifts. I write to Aleksandar, tell him he should come visit. Check the time. Stare at the screen.

Else is thirty-two; long face, long teeth, long hair. Even her eyes droop. Clothes hang off her like they don't want to be there; this isn't what the manufacturers promised. I look stout beside her, beside everyone here. She links me in a way I'm not used to, like someone grabbing a bag strap on the way out of a burning building. And then we're off, before I have time to wonder, usually to a bar or a café, because we don't know what else there is. She talks, doesn't stop talking, that's what I love, the noise that keeps on coming, the endless variations. Her accent. The proximity of that voice to my ears. I don't want her to ever stop talking, telling me what it all looks like, telling me about the north, about the chain of islands up there that drip into the sea. I want to squeeze her body like a tin of spinach until the contents pop out of her and into me. I don't tell her this exactly, but she links my arm and runs and I break into a corresponding sprint.

The whole city a treadmill splashed with water and floodlights. Snowflakes schmoozing downward. Running into Wim and Anouk, into their two linked arms and down onto the snow piles. Our hapless faces peeking out of the cold low melting sides. Flapping our legs and arms to leave a friendly mark for the next in line. They are fifty-six years each, primarily silver hair and dark grey creases. Tobacco colours and narrow ridges line the grain of their thick fingernails. Hands like dying trees. There is no part of their bodies that has not already learnt something. I remember the day I noticed

DISTANT HILLS

the skin between my top knuckles and cuticles, how it had changed texture: shattered glass, a million nearly imperceptible fragments. Triangulation. I'd seen it in others, and now here it was, it had happened to me. I wanted to tell people, tried. It didn't have much of an effect. I remember an ex-boyfriend who tucked his first grey hair into the Velcro of his wallet to take it home and show his friends.

Anouk and Wim cook us homemade pasta when we go round to their damp apartment for dinner. Trails of dough sliming out of that machine when they twist and yank its handle. Dropping down the side of the kitchen counter and into the bowl on the floor. We drink red wine out of enormous glasses, smiling like we all think this is the size glasses should be. This is what we do, this is how we speak. Grinning around the table, cheeks all glowing embers as we articulate our needs, about films and travel and bits of history we have read about inside in-flight magazines. Picking the pasta up with long metal tong ends. Clumps of pesto holding on as we mountain-rescue it as it waves back to its loved ones still down in the pit, rising, rising up on each pasta string. Eyes that beam and beam and arms that nudge and link and sometimes go around the shoulder. Bodies that sway and suggest things. I want to get drunk and sleep in a pile and say sorry and stay there forever, clinking ribs, sweat diluting. Evaporating, becoming clouds again. More than one hundred years between them: Anouk and Wim.

I remember all their faces, I know who is next and what they want to drink. They think I'm Irish, some of them; it helps with the tips. When I smile I get my teeth out and dome my eyelids. I do the sums in my head on the way to the till. Else often comes in, glad to have got out of here, can't believe how much time she's wasted in this place, seriously: orders a drink. She's wearing an eighties fluorescent-pink head band, black sweat band on her left wrist, bright pink trainers with glow-in-the-dark stripes and laces. Drinking a fruity cider with neon-green painted nails wiping the rim. She's putting a deep red colour onto her lips, looking around. At Wim and Anouk and Jaap, and that guy with the saliva in the crook of his mouth, the one with the slight limp; at the woman whose trousers are always a little too low not to be persistently leered at; and at the one with the cigarette holder and the strained eyes who is always sniffling into some book in the corner. They are all here, this is the centre of the world. This is where I dropped the pin.

Aleksandar's coming! Says he's lonely there, that he'll never amount to anything. Says if I don't mind him staying, if Jaap doesn't mind him staying, he'll come visit for a few days, maybe a week, maybe two. I text him back immediately and tell him to advance, that the route to the north is clear. All morning I flit around, pond skater in a padded coat. Barely opening the doors to shops, barely touching coins as I pluck them from my barely open wallet, barely picking up my barely dropped hat. I look up at that clock tower where all the roads collide, all five, where nobody is sure where to look next and nobody is certain who has right of way. Those cables that tell the trams which way to go, an infinite mystic rose etched into a barely blue sky. That arch you can run under to get to the shopping street a little faster, only to not remember why you were in such a rush to get there anyway. Roads you can't cross. Bicycles you don't hear coming. Angry bells announcing perfectly justified frowning faces.

DISTANT HILLS

Back-pedalling. Moon-walking your way out of the line of fire. Saying sorry, because that's the same in both languages. Doing prayer shapes with hands that don't know any better gesture yet. Aleksandar's coming, so now the crowd divides into three categories: locals, tourists, and him.

Else, I grab her. Genuine. Without hesitation. Just grab her body and tug it towards mine and stifle. Her top and bottom ends bulging slightly, a wheeze escaping from the central third. *Aleksandar's coming!* I say.

'Who?' she asks. Eyebrows—two pauses that should not be there.

'I told you. In Croatia. My friend. With the doll. Zlat's friend. Zlat, the guy I was with. I told you.'

'Right,' she says, eyes drooping. Unconvincing, unconvinced. 'That's really good news. Want to go for a drink?'

And I think I do. My heart, or whereabouts I perceive it, feels expansive, all the layers of body around it swelling out. There is so much blood inside this skin. I walk with Else, between the parked, unparked, or abandoned bicycles, giving a little skip each time the paving slabs fail to meet. I want to press my swollen chest into the other pedestrians, crushing them with it into the art-deco facades of passing cinemas. Then I want to turn them around and lift their tops up and admire the elaborate inverse print.

The world shrinks down to Aleksandar, to this new point of focus. All the hands of all the clocks turn and point to him: a series of lines in one-point perspective. I raise a mighty glass and laugh. Only my laughing mouth has any meaning. Else's face and the wallpaper of whatever bar this is and its fleur-de-lis pattern smudge to grey. I clink her glass, because no one wants to be left hanging for too long, and she co-clinks mine because it both looks and feels okay. We're out, we're about, and this is really happening. This is real, authentic vigour. Beer turns to gold inside us and our blood boils and burns and runs half-marathons through our melee.

I arm-wrestle this little country under the table. I look every single one of this city's proponents in their two eyes until they too blink out of my life; turning into the blundering criminals of unidentified shop aisles on the grainy footage of unwatched CCTV. I *am* Amsterdam, just like all the signs told me I would be; and Else is not, not really, because I can't get inside her, can't get past the nail paint and the headband and all that trailing-off eyeliner, can't see what she's thinking or what she's about to say when she almost does and then in the end she doesn't; and Aleksandar is coming to me.

'I want to go home,' I tell Jaap. Two clickety wrists try to catch me from falling over. My eyes exactly the same as always except they're not even in the room or in my head or attached to a single word I say. They don't look at Jaap because that's impossible but they look around where they think he might be, and focus at near enough the correct height and distance. Then if anybody asks I can confidently evidence my intentions at least.

'Take me home.'

Stumble.

'Jaap?'

And I don't know what I'm looking at. Can't move. Any further exertion will result in nothing, cause it all to fall to smithereens. Better to stay fully immersed in this present position, just stay like this until somebody notices I can't do a thing about it. I don't have the assertiveness required, the piece of paper that says I should, should, shouldn't. I cannot move. Cannot look Jaap or any other object in its eye or nearest side. Wait. The creaks, wind, the endless drumroll. And Jaap doing nothing, saying nothing, waiting to go away. If he lets go now I will fall to the floor and never move again. Then he'll see, in the morning, after his nice cool sleep, when I am still lying there crumpled, crooked limbs and potential pool of my own urine soaking into his nice smooth varnished floorboards. Then he'll do something, then he'll act. Saying *Oh sorry, I didn't realise, didn't realise that you meant it, that it was serious.* But I could not be making this any clearer. It could not be any more obvious that I would not have stopped moving if I still had any choice.

Turns out my silence does not speak volumes, that it in fact says very little. The perfect noise to sleep through, soothing as whale song. Look at it carefully for a few moments, give it a little prod, weigh up the likelihood of anything further happening, and then go to bed. That's it, world; that's the one. I'll stand here until I die, and then some, until some bit of me dies and somebody finally clears away the scrap heap. Jaap will move out and others will move in and I'll still be standing here, or lying in a ball down there, estate agent kicking my clothes into a smaller heap and excusing the décor. They won't get a rise out of me, they can do what they like, they can set me on fire.

Jaap walks me backward to the couch, guides me down gently into a foetal shape with a few firm forearm manoeuvres. Like five-point parking a rusty wheelbarrow. Covers me in the two rarely washed living-room blankets. Furls one up and under my lifeless chin. Sets things straight. I dream in headaches, falling in and out of forgotten domains.

Else calls in the morning. Says that last night I was finger-swearing at every man over forty in the room. Last thing she saw of me I was waving at her as I scooted past on the back of someone else's motorbike, both legs hanging off the same side, arms slicing the air. The thing about Amsterdam is the streets are all so beautiful and narrow, strings of pretty little lights dotted about the sky, that you think nothing can go wrong here when you enter from outside, when you drink your beer in its specific fancy glass and forget to cry. Or, when the tears do fall, you tell people (and yourself) it's because the aesthetics of the place are so damn charming. And it might be. Tears of beauty, that's all. A natural waste product of being alive.

Else wants to come over but I don't let her. Wants to sit on Jaap's couch or Jaap's floor, drinking my teabags left floating in Jaap's cups in their isolated ponds of hot water. Wants to talk about whatever until neither of us ever gets anywhere. Else is looking for work. I'm looking for different work. I tell her it's not a good idea to come round this time. My phone beeps. A text from the motorbike man. Turns out I stuck my thumb into the middle of the road, he unrevved his engine, stopped, and brought me home. He asks if I want to go for coffee or maybe, just maybe, a beer. Tells me I seemed pretty distressed last night, while we were sat outside on the wall in front of my (i.e. Jaap's) apartment. News to me. I go to the window, look out. Sure enough, pretty accommodating wall out there standing neatly under a finely angled street light. Seems a viable location for such a scene. I delete the message. Don't need to know.

DISTANT HILLS

When Kathy had her first baby I was staying with a friend in a village on the outskirts of Belgrade. Eating abstract meat and wearing an old lady's house shoes. Me and the lady didn't understand each other much, smiling and nodding and pointing at things that might be of note. One morning, over Turkish coffee, her eyes lit up and she grabbed my arm. Tugged me outside to the garden. *She's showing you her chickens*, my friend, her youngest son, said. *Her pets*. Okay, I thought. Cool. She took me to a kind of shed or utility room. Hundreds of feathery bony deformations, huge eyes, pathetic bald necks stretched out through the railings. My friend's mother looked so happy, so excited. *Eggs!* she said in English, nodding proudly and waving her arm.

That house in the village on the outskirts of Belgrade was three stories high: grandparents on the bottom, parents in the middle, sons at the top. They built an extra floor each time a new generation came along, stacked them all up. The family also had a dog. Apparently it used to live in the house until the top-floor son, the one who had remained at home, undisturbed by the size of the world or by its photographic representations, got a wife and a baby. I saw that dog every morning and every night, running perfect circles in the snow. Brown arc on white. Wooden post tied to a chain. Simple maths. Every couple of rotations trying to sit down and then failing because of the cold.

Kathy's baby was three months old when I met it. Other than the fact itself and what I've since seen on photographs, I don't really remember. I remember walking around a fort in Novi Sad. I remember trains. I do know about the feeling of a baby's hand clutched around an index finger. That much I do know. The last time I took a night train I spent most of the journey waking and sweating and imagining the train was crashing, going off the rails. That never used to happen. I used to revel in it, the lostness. I used to feel safe.

I've already told Else a lot of the basic stories. She knows about Kathy and Zlat and a string of my usual official anecdotes; the crowd pleasers, ones I've shaped to perfection. The well-timed punchlines, truisms, turning points, all that. She's got my biog. and I've got hers. We'd easily pass the *How Well Do You Really Know The Person You're About To Marry?* quiz. Easily. Surname: Heijman; age: 32; siblings: one, male, older, married; favourite food: gnocchi; favourite animal: moose; favourite letter: *F*; favourite Dutch word: Scheveningen; favourite English word: *cranky*. If Else was an independent state, I'd be granted citizenship, no problem. But right now, I want to see if Kathy has emailed, and look for work.

Kathy has replied. She is also online, which is better for me because I don't need to pre-think a full reply. She tells me the due date, asks when I'm coming home, says that if it's not before then, it would be really nice if I could orchestrate a visit around that time. I tell her that it totally depends on my work situation, that I'm hoping to find something a lot more permanent soon, and that I'm feeling quite positive about it. She understands, she says. She pastes a list of potential names into the chat window and asks me if I want to help choose one. All the names sound the same to me, so I tell her to trust her instinct and not to rush any decisions and that when it comes out and she holds it she'll know. I give myself a nod and look around to my imagined supporters (all of whom are smiling and whooping at me) because that seems to really be the best thing a person could have replied with in this particular situation. She's happy. I'm happy. Despite the knocking in my head.

DISTANT HILLS

I allow myself a break from that exertion before I get down to the bulk of the job search. I shower, start to dry, think better of it. I make sure the door to the flat is locked, turn the heating up full whack, and go natural. Nice to air-dry once in a while; saves the towel. Nice to feel the warm wind blow through all your cleaves. Touching. Cold floor, bare feet. Slap, slap, slap, slap. Turn the music up loud so the world becomes less boisterous. Spin, breathe, spin. Breathe.

Picture of Jaap as a child on the fridge. Picture of a child that must be Jaap on a shelf by the music-making machine. I pseudo-foxtrot to the kitchen where I take a cup from the sink and smash it on the ground. A pause. Consider the wreckage. No idea how that happened. I touch my hands together like mirror images, with just the fingertips touching, the way politicians get trained at hand school. Fingertip to corresponding fingertip. Fingers impacting against each other. I am still here.

I put some clothes on and clean up the mess. Squatting but not kneeling, in case of shard in knee. I ring Else. Hang up before she picks up. Heat some water, make some coffee, drink some coffee, look out the window, heat some water, make some coffee, go for a wee. I ring Else. I hang up. I take my clothes off, put on a T-shirt, head-push my way into the middle of the bedsheets. 13:28.

Fuck this, I think. I call Else. 'What are you doing? Me too. Same, same. Do you want to go somewhere? Does it matter? Yeah I'm feeling, so ... so ... so ... yeah like jumpy, grabby, restless, yeah, antsy, no, no, not like angst, yeah. Cool. Let's do it. Meet you on Kinkerstraat. Fifteen.'

Else looks like she's been crying, but I don't ask her about it and she doesn't say anything. She stares at me a little more intensely than she might usually, to see if I'm eyeing at her unordinarily in any way. To see if I'm looking at the rash of pink around her over-emphasised three-dimensional eye space. I want to poke one, watch it spring. Of course I'm looking at her in the regular fashion, it's her thoughts that are staring—that's what she forgets. It's the guilty that stare at the innocent to check how they are being received.

    My brazen palm connects to her brazen palm and our fingers interlace habitually. I'm a top-thumber with my right hand and an underthumb with my left. We swing our connecting arms in the hope that something like the mood rubs off on us.

V.

I AM STANDING in the long corridor that runs beneath the platforms at Centraal Station. I waited here yesterday for three long hours and Aleksandar didn't come. His phone wasn't working or he had my number wrong, and after scanning and swiping at every face coming at me from the distance for a large part of what was then my future, I got home to check my emails and thereupon learnt his train had been delayed. Meaning the long-haul sleeper carriage from Zagreb couldn't connect to its connection in time to complete the course, and Aleksandar had determined it wiser to return to the town from which he came, send me an email, have a relaxing evening, and tomorrow (today) begin again.

Of course, it was my fault. I should have checked my emails before I went to bed. The message was there, waiting. Disappointment is often a feeling you do to yourself. It wouldn't exist if we didn't keep hoping for things, expecting the future to happen like a foregone arrangement. I made myself traipse out, dressed as neatly as I could muster, into the rain or the fog or whatever the weather was doing around my emotions. Made myself stand there grinning, staring up at the platform steps, trying to see the highest step I could without crouching down on my knees in the middle of a crowd side-to-siding me with their own crowd-based preoccupations. Trying to make him come faster. Guessing the trainers, the gallops, waiting for a face waiting for mine.

It could all have been avoided. If I'd only had the rationality to check my correspondence, to remember that it is uncertainty that causes belief. I do it to myself, I know, by wanting to be this pathetic thing that flounders, waiting to be scraped off the underside of some rock and deemed viable, worthy of inspection. I want to be justified. I want to inflict pain and further pain upon myself while at the same time standing there laughing at the (lack of) results. I want the experience and also the spectacle of that experience. Like when Zlat pushed the door into me—I watched myself hunched over, folded up, wondering if I might actually do myself some real damage with all that tearing up of my ribs and lungs and stomach acid. Purposefully creasing and exhausting their capacity. I watched myself standing in Jaap's living room, drunk, imagining how easy it would be to speak, to move, to say, *sorry, don't know what that was all about. As you were.* Easy yet impossible. Unwanted.

I stood in the train station yesterday both hoping he would and also hoping he would not come. Hoping to be destroyed a little bit so I could stop trying to look so okay. Hoping to achieve an extreme.

I should have checked my emails, this could all have been avoided. Still, nobody tried to hurt me and no one was hurt; nothing but another forgiveable, forgettable human mistake. I was working late at the Irish bar, making plenty of tips, the customers were friendly,

DISTANT HILLS

the roads were clear. Two Belgian beers in my belly and that rising feeling like a gannet coming up for air. That swoop. I was soaring along the smooth roads on my bicycle, had it all together, no pains in my knees, hands exactly where they were supposed to be, pedals under my complete control. Should have checked my emails when I got back to Jaap's apartment instead of scrolling through old pictures of Croatia on my phone.

'Hey, Saturn!' And two arms clasp me like I'm vital, levitate me to the next wall-tile up. Ice rings shatter. I'm Neptune, I'm anything.

'Mercury!' I cry. 'Finally! I've been waiting here since yesterday morning. Slept right there (points) under that stray coffee cup. It was okay but a bit of a drip from the ceiling, bit of a milky smell to the room, you know, dried lipstick on the sheets, and so on. Still, good location. Overall, a thumbs up.'

Aleksandar turns one of his eyes into a tiny slit and pulls his best magnifying-glass face at me with the other, grinning. Tells me his horse is undergoing rigorous quarantine inspections at the German border and we will need to take the tram.

'Drink first?' I suggest. 'Before I take you to the palace?'

After Aleksandar has finished gawping at all the beer names, both at their quantity and their spelling, we finally clink glasses and click back into place.

'Zlat's married.'

'Huh?'

'Yeah, thought you should know.'

'It's only been six months!'

'Yeah. I think they already for long time know each other.'

'Right.'

There are certain moments that are similar to obsessively refreshing internet pages and hoping something comes of it. Sipping my beer approximately every fifteen seconds, flicking my beer mat against the edge of the table. I'm hoping Aleksandar will say something else, move me along, take me to a place louder and more mindful than here. My brain rattles around like the sound of parents sobbing in adjacent rooms throughout long young darknesses, a sound you can't ignore but have no authority to try to change. An infinite camera zoom, a falling dream, waking up in a stranger's room again. I'm sitting among Italy's ruins as the final cultural artefact is routinely destroyed, staring at tourists making *V*s with their fingers and taking the same photograph again and again. I'm the bricked-up lost cause in the old Pagan wall. History's paralysis. Cause and effect. What if I free myself and it all comes apart?

'Sorry,' Aleksandar says.

'How long are you staying?' I ask.

'Five days. Why?'

Aleksandar's arms around me. Binary stars.

Jaap's invited everyone over for dinner: Anouk, Wim, Else, Aleksandar and me. It's almost convincing. We're sat in two neat lines, three by three. The extra chairs are out, the heating is on low. So many bodies bristling. Somehow we're all waiting for our turn to speak. I'm sobbing gently deep inside the last natural annex of myself, holding my chest in, pinning my feet to the ground with my hands on my knees. Else is jovial, regaling us with stories of when she was backpacking through Vietnam, the trivial errors she made. Her teeth are beautiful, two perfect walls, a portcullis slamming down between each chord. And Aleksandar's eyes are shining, two

DISTANT HILLS

beaming space ships trying to make contact, to understand.

Anouk stands, a graceful grey plant stretching up towards the light. Tendrils of long hair seeking softer ground. She's a mangrove, a strangler fig, a slow and welcome threat, while I'm the pole of a fence, roughly cut, lacking context, man-made. If only I could be sure age would be like that, delicate and certain as the oscillations of a murmured soundwave fading out to silence. A harmony of space. The way certain songs end. Jaap's behind me; he's got his two hands vicing on my shoulders. I'm rising, rising, a bubble of gas beneath his fine palm ceiling. My body stutters, relaxes, and does not float away.

There is always sadness, it exists behind everything, like mice in the walls, intermittently dying but never cleared away. Like the glazed moments glimpsed between the animations of Wim's busy face. Sometimes, like now, that sadness feels okay. There is no line between misery and happiness, it's all there at the same time, a kind of radiation shooting through the structure of things; penetrating, entering, altering, passing through. Something like happiness is in me now, there's something surging. I'm welling like the tide of the sea. My happiness is bursting with the pain of not being able to touch it, share it, scream at everyone in the room that this is actually the moment. That this really is the one.

VI.

AND THERE IT is, I'm holding it. The one part of nature we haven't quite managed to quit or control yet. A free sample: a new human, a new time scale. Another set of eyes to eventually look at us like all we are is the sum of the mistakes we have collectively made.

Kathy is melting at me because I am considering her baby, which is another way of considering her, her extended achievements. Another way of eliminating doubt. I hold it like a cat, with its paws up. Looking at it ignoring me. Oblivion. *Forgetting* as the state from which we are made.

'Do you want to stay here tonight? You're more than welcome. There might be some crying but she's been quite good these last few weeks.'

'Not really, no. I'm not sleeping well at the moment. Tend to get up and walk around a lot. Think it's better if I go.'

'You okay? Are you going to go back to Amsterdam?'

'Don't know. I only booked one flight.'

DISTANT HILLS

'Do you want another cup of tea?'
'Yeah, okay.'

Kathy and I met back when we were still routinely forgetting most of everything; so we'll always be around, like water or walls, just a couple of nondescript landmarks that are frequently trod into ground. Like an old house you might have lived in, which, if nearby, you'll always detour past to see if it's still standing. Kathy's living in her big house with her big kids and her big husband, and it's all so very sound. Whereas I? I'm something more ephemeral except without the beauty which that word implies. I'm something more transient except without the ability to really truly disappear.

Kathy tells me Dean and Mona have moved in together. Solid. The way people cling like damp rags and then harden in the sun. Waves come crashing overhead but I hold my valuables just above the water line and clench the gleaming splash-soaked rock with fingers surprised they can still hang on. Of course, Dean and Mona are nothing to me, periphery, but still one notices when the pieces move on. When pedestrians hole themselves up between their brick-blocked neighbours, draw their curtains, and line their smooth cream walls with framed photographs of their own young faces in the great outdoors where their legs jump high high high above the restrictive ground of this too-small planet in vintage chiffon.

Kathy brings in the hot tea and looks at me through the baby and the steam. We used to be the same age. Something happened. I miss her terribly, but there's no reason to stay. We have nothing to say that can't be said via email. Occasionally I return and hold a child for a moment or two, and look at it and show my face.

Else hung herself. That's the real reason I came back. Everywhere you go it's all the same. No one wants to be where they are, with who they're standing next to. I didn't tell Kathy, she wouldn't have known what it meant to me anyway. It was early in the morning, after the party while Aleksandar was visiting, which resulted in his leaving early. Couldn't hack it. Went to Eindhoven. Double whammy. We've barely spoken since. A couple of apologetic and a couple of angry emails. What else is there to say?

Mercury rising. It's almost summer again and I have nowhere to be, no tan line waiting for me. Memories of skinny-dipping on a beach in Bulgaria is all I'll have to look back on, the hugeness of sand and the walls so pink and sky in the world. Clouds in my eyes and stolen cameras and being carried off of public toilets with my trousers down because I've fallen asleep in the thick of it all one more time.

I thought Aleksandar and Else were part of a proper collection, thought they'd go down in history with me. However, we collide artificially and at rapid speeds. She left no note, no text, no email. Petered out in a haze of hopeful red-wine glory, while I was telling Wim and Anouk how much their relationship meant to me. Took her leap of faith and swung away. I received the news by text message from the manager of the Irish bar; turns out suicide admin got their ropes crossed and thought that Else still worked there. Must be hard to make sense of an alphabetical list of an ex-correspondent's SIM-carded first names.

No amount or variation of Queen lyrics could break through the bass tones of wailing that I was shedding that morning. Layers of irreversibility. Nothing really matters. Aleksandar doing air guitar

DISTANT HILLS

because we're just not used to realness. *Are you going to take me home tonight?* Aleksandar was singing, right arm crashing down post-arc to tremble against six almost-strings. *Are you going to let it all hang out? I've been with you such a long time, you're my sunshine. Ooh, you make me live.* Until he looked up at me and realised then wasn't the time and there wasn't the place.

Kathy re-hands me the cup of tea and I focus in on the confused and concerned look she's giving me, wondering if her current expression is a regular thing baby-number-latest has to see, or if this particular emotion is just between us.

Burning through the sky, I'm having such a good time. Don't stop me, don't stop me, I don't want to stop at all.

'Well, the offer's always there. You know you're welcome to stay any time.'

I collect my things—jacket, phone, rucksack—and I'm out the welcoming door.

I walk the eight miles to the city centre; dual carriageway escorting me along the length of its packed-out vein. I needed the space, wanted to feel the achievement of manipulating air with my own body. However, my feet are flat and increasingly unsuitable, my lower back curves painfully around the underside of my pack, the cars exhaust me. Watching their progress and then watching my own pathetic body that isn't even capable of being a proper beast of burden, that can't even transport my own possessions down some smooth flat road. Under an overpass, out of sight somewhat but not entirely, I submit to my knees, to the weakness of joints and temporary connections, and cry into the graffitied concrete that tries to console me by shouting PIGS and ADAM and ROZ and FUCK CAPITALISM and PATRICK SCUM ARLO JAKE AND THE CREW BASTARDS PENIS FUCK OFF.

VII.

BLACK-AND-WHITE posters of New Romantics blu-tacked to the walls. A low-hanging shadeless lightbulb brazenly boasting its minimal filament. Pockmarks where old posters were, craters where layers of paint have been adhesived away; tiny dancers flashing bright white against tobacco-beige. My nose one sharp inhale away from a nostrilful of ash and filter. I move the ashtray off the bed and smell the pillow and try to work out what this means for me today.

It is 13:12. Head like a boiling kettle whose switch is kaput. A low whistle and the sound of water turning to steam. Damo saunters in with his nipples out and a tall glass of what looks like it might be wine in his left hand and I'm starting to put a situation to this scene.

'How's it going this morning?' Damo asks.

'Afternoon, no?'

'Right, yeah.'

'I'm okay. I think.'

'You were pretty rough last night. Told me about your mate, Elle, who took a jump . . .'

'Else.'

'Right. Anyway, you need a drink?'

'Wine? Not really.'

'A mouthful'll sort you out.'

'Nah, I'm okay.'

Damo tells me how I fell asleep during each of the three films we spent last night watching. How I woke up, whimpered a little, drank a little, explained why I was whimpering a little, and then fell back to sleep. I apologise for calling on him unannounced and he lights a cigarette and says it is always nice to hear from me and goes to the fridge to fetch himself a beer.

Me and Damo used to live together in a flatshare with a couple of other friends or acquaintances in a big old house, since converted into what might now be stylish apartments, on a grotty old litter-backed street. Damo's room smells of unwashed linen and forgotten corners, his body shimmers through a fine layer of human grease. It's hard to imagine why I thought this was the refuge I should come to, that this was the boost I could need. Damo drags the cover off me, tells me I'm letting the day get away, laughs and retreats to his convex computer screen.

Travelling at the speed of light, Aleksandar had sorted me out, ordered us pizzas, and fled for the most convenient train. Broccoli, olives and green peppers expanded and contracted before me as I pushed down mouthfuls of pizza and tears as I blinked and frowned. Said he had to be on his own, far from this event, needed to process it, had never known anyone take away their own life be-

67

fore, needed to think about that. Sooner the better, he said, lest it affect him without his realising how and why certain changes within himself were happening. For his horse I gave him some not-quite-fresh apples, which had been sitting around in my (Jaap's) not-quite-salad-bowl for some days, and he smiled at me like the past was done with, and I was a fool for not being up to speed.

Kathy texts to ask if I'm okay and I say to Damo, 'Fuck it, pass me a wine.'

Two wines down and me and Damo are doing charcoal drawings in the park nearby on A3 watercolour paper. I'm trying to draw Dasha in the sea, perfect ovals around her, rippling. The water acknowledging her weight, making a little space. Lace patterns. Water moving into the transparencies around her flower-dashed sleeves. A perfect mould. The way we don't make doilies any longer. I bet she embroiders. I bet she sits out on her balcony on a striped fold-away chair with an organic facemask cleansing her pores. I bet the sun illuminates every angle of her face with 3D-scan precision, recording her absolute selfhood on the memory of the world forever.

I'm drawing her in the sea, from the chest up, hovering like a gem, like a thing that knows what effort went into forming it and where it should be. Like amber on a beach. Like a treasure that knows people will be combing every inch of the earth for a glimpse of it. A rock of amber gently dusted over with sand, happy to wait a million years basking in occasional shivers of sunlight and splashes of sea. A rock of amber happy to wait, knowing that if it isn't found and granted value, it will continue to lie there shimmering regardless and eventually become another thing.

'Who's that?' asks Damo.

'Friend of an ex I don't see anymore. What's yours?'

Damo shows me his paper. Robocop attending a therapy session; his record bag placed by the side of his chair depicted in cross-section-reveal, full of stolen ketchup and malt-vinegar sachets.

The sun's starting to run out and my shoulders are thankfully turning pink; a little bit of something, at least. Proof I've appreciated the season's first attempts at heat. I leave the picture of Dasha on a park bench, as it doesn't really resemble her anyway. My hands and cheeks are charcoal-black. I'm happy enough for the moment, so let's leave it at that, as one of those objects people find as interludes to their otherwise predictable days.

We walk over the endless grass to the endless gates, and on, past the endless pavement to the endless bus stop. The wine sprouting fresh warmth and completeness in my veins. Hard amber. I will continue to contain everything I contain.

We go to a gig and it's sort of perfect. A dark room full of bodies to press against me. A pack. A group of people who want to be by my side. Damo's face spotlit in the crowd, holding high a fluorescent cider for me, and it's all so nostalgic and the stage lights shine through the bubbles through the plastic and I take a sip and it's both unpleasant and terribly comforting and I remember falling in love here once. Remember standing side by side in the darkness that live music provides, with the tiniest of spaces between the boldest of unsure fingers. I remember a shoulder level with my ear and a presence like the North Pole; static as eventually claiming something. A reference point, a safe base to explore from.

DISTANT HILLS

That was before I left the first time. Before my personal event horizon started fizzing up and I started flying out and falling in to countries I didn't know the shapes of yet and wanted to grab with stronger hands.

He came to visit me in Poland. I hated the way he sang to himself as he walked across my apartment, hated the hair on his knuckles, hated his overstated-understated socks. I called it off via videochat after he left, after two rage-muffled weeks of dinners and walks and conversations about how to pick this up again properly once I came home. But I didn't come home. I went back to where I'd started for a while, much like now, except for new bridges being erected across old railway lines and new towers prodding the sky. He'd taken me seriously and moved on, got together with someone more his type, and so, predictably, I became impossibly in love with his reality's demise.

And so here, in sweat-heavy compact rooms with unowned limbs almost everywhere idly touching, I remember. Not the hairs popping out from an infuriation of pores, but a togetherness in uncertain gestures, a slow approach, and the unquestionable and unwavering purpose of fixation that fills and floods the mind.

Damo looms in and tries to kiss me but I tell him I'm not here for that, I just wanted to spend some time with a familiar face for a while. He's unfazed and raises his half-full plastic pint at mine.

'Cheers mate! Great sound!' and he's dancing away again.

I'm staring at the lighting technicians' ceiling work and feeling the reverb rising up from my toes into my contents and am swaying into anyone that will have me for the moment. He's here, Mr. Poland, I know it, he always is. I can't stay. I can't ever stay. Every unknown male in the room possesses his face.

Damo takes me to his friend's house en route home. Hours die around me in a repetition of whiskey capsules and apparently hilarious face shapes. In endless things said and immediately evaporated. In the wiping out of the trivia of one moment in order to better be there in the following one, the present one, this one, this one right here, again and again. We're singing, of course we are, and it's out of time, but we're all in it together, whoever we are. Damo takes me to his friend's house and I wake up some unknown day later in Damo's bed again, with my face up against the ashtray and my mouth dry as space-food and Damo walks in with his nipples out and a tall glass of what might be wine in his left hand and he says *morning* and I say *afternoon*.

VIII.

I'M WORKING AT a campsite in the Peak District. I brought my two-man tent and the owners said I can pitch the entire season out in any undesirable corner I feel like. Nothing uphill, nowhere with a view, neither too near nor too far from the toilets. I heeled my pegs down through the moist earth near a scrappy line of hedgerow and a thick oak's trunk; not too perfect, not too grim.

Martha is the campsite owner, and her husband Roy comes and goes and chucks fresh bread and homemade shortcake out of his slid-down window at the front of my tent every other morning as he drives off-site. Inside, my backpack is down on its side to create a kind of off-ground shelf; tops, bottoms and sundries in three piles across its length. Dirty clothes go back inside the pack, along with spare books, and anything I either don't need to access very often or don't want to get damp. Shoes near the door on a flattened-out piece of cardboard, toiletries in the side pocket—toothbrush in the middle, two bottles of water near the rolled-up jumper for a pillow that supports my head, and, hanging from a cord in the middle of the inner layer's underside, a swinging light.

It's cosy. Everything is accessible without needing to compromise one's centre of gravity. You find yourself a spot, bed down, and live. Stretching your arms and mouth and legs. There's a plastic bag filled with non-perishables and, in the porch, another filled with waste. I pull the zip of the sleeping bag up to the bottom of my face. I'm going back inside, into the bowels of this fabric, my feet pushing down towards the end of the line. It's all been worked out. Everything knows where it should be. My phone lives in the zip-down top pocket of the bag, in its own little tucked-away bed. The computer sleeps in the backpack's back-supporting metal-lined document pocket. I click off the head-torch hanging from the dome ceiling, place my book in the book-shaped space beyond the rolled-up-jumper, lie on my back and wait until the seams of the tent appear in the immediately fading black of the eye-adjusted moonlit night. A domain the same size as an arm span, me squared; it's enough to manage.

Often I'm left on the campsite alone as Martha goes off visiting friends, running errands, promoting embroidery and holistic therapies. Often I'm left on the campsite alone as the tents are packed up and the eggshells emptied and the bacon shrivelled and eaten well before 9 a.m. Then there's just an eternity of myself to get through before the round of 2 p.m. wet boots arrive and pitch up and check in. Occasionally, either side of noon, as I'm weeding or reading or putting off cleaning the toilets, I hear a sheepish zip, see a flustered face glance hesitantly at the sky, watch it retreat.

I've been drinking with Daniel and Casey the past two nights, over

DISTANT HILLS

by their flame-throwing bonfire and bed-bulged van.

'You work here?!' (Casey)

'No way!' (Daniel)

'As if. We had no idea.'

'That explains why you didn't want to come to the caves with us yesterday.'

'You should have come though. Have you been yet? You drive? They're fantastic.'

'And so close!'

'Do you get time off? We're heading up to Scotland for a month or so in a couple of days.'

'Best thing we ever bought, this van, isn't it, Case? This van? Remember?'

'I can't believe you work here. So cool. You must get days off. She didn't check us in, right? Dan? It was that man. With the hat, yeah? Yeah, those caves are really cool. Deep . . .' She winks.

I'm drinking a bottle of red wine, and the weight of it in my hand, of my holding it—the dimensions. The piece of wood I'm sitting on. The complete heaviness pooling within me as I swallow this liquid. So very much a thing, this bottle. Pure evening-field moisture is soaking politely through the fronts of my shoes. Casey and Daniel are from Tulsa, Oklahoma, and I just keep staring at them. I don't know much else; I'm not sure I've been asking them anything, or even if I'm interested. It's enough just to watch their faces flap about and see our head-torches and the tips of passing flames reflect in the windows of their van and the glimmers of their eyes.

It's enough to look. I watch Daniel and Casey like watching aeroplanes from a viewing lounge, knowing at some point I should do something or go somewhere, but not now, not yet; just one more. I want to see one more land home safely. I need to be sure.

I take my laptop down the lane to one of the village's WiFi-enabled cafes and there it is, an email from Kathy. I've hardly spoken to her since the day I refused her offer of a place to stay. We met up in a country park one afternoon since then; I lasted about four hours, she said I was distant and that she was finding it hard to connect with me. I played hide-and-seek with two of her children and avoided any sort of a reply.

Kathy's email tells me she's heard I've been hanging around with Damo again and she's worried about me and I'm irresponsible and I really should get in touch with my parents. And when did I last see them? And where am I now anyway? And what am I playing at? And why haven't I been answering her calls?

I stayed at Damo's for two weeks or more and drank too much too cheaply and saw the sun at the wrong end of the day, and the moon when the sun should have been coming back again. I know why she's angry, but I'm less sure why she thinks it might be useful. We're never going to swap places, me and Kathy, to understand various and substantial things about one another's lives. Some people pull a certain face when you open up to them—one that's almost blank and thinks itself neutral, but that largely wants the conversation to stop, the explanations and self-consideration to not be happening; wants the visible desperation more cloaked, more shattered. Tiny harmless bite-size cubes, portions to be taken with water, blended in amongst the mashed potatoes, nudged away.

Kathy's email can't be replied to. There is no answer to any of her questions that will not bifurcate into further questions. Plus, any answer I give her will likely be made up anyway. I don't know, but to tell her I don't know is an admission of defeat, like passing a move, swapping your tiles. When any kind of two-point score would be better employed. I mark the email unread with the intention of reading it again and replying later but I presume I never will.

Instead I read through some of Else's last texts, which is a bad habit I've come into since leaving Damo's place, since sobering up slightly instead of sinking my head in a previous decade: adopting Bargain-Booze alternatives to time travel, re-watching black-and-white cult classics, re-playing 16-bit computer games. I didn't tell Jaap I might not be back, just took what I needed and said I would be gone for a while. He seemed indifferent anyway, was putting clean sheets on the bed I had been using as I was leaving for the plane. We gave each other an awkward hug, sincere but unwanted, both playing the parts of age-old acquaintances with no hesitation concerning the act of physical embrace.

'Let's join a class,' said Else, 'yoga or pole or something. I need to jump around.'

I met Zlat down on the beach on the afternoon I arrived in the town where he lived. Backpack under my head, and feet enjoying the substance from which the ground is made. Seemed almost impossible, the way after a week of purposeless train travel, my future might just be okay. The world might just keep on surprising me if I continued to let myself be shunted around, if I trusted in its motions. A week after standing in the dust by the road in Armenia, my stomach tight as diamonds, seeing nothing but trouble and imminent reprisal, I'd somehow navigated the timetables, the maps and the distance, and fallen upon this what-looked-like-gold.

And now married. Six months. It amazes me the things people get done.

I look out the cafe windows, over the rolling hills, over the receding steam of my cooling coffee, and wonder if this is a moment I'm likely to remember; this campsite, this summer. Will I make myself proud? Will Casey and Dan tell a single story about me to anyone? 'You're not *that* young,' Roy said to me, not long after I arrived at reception with a finger already pointed at the *Staff Sought* sign, when he and Martha were settling me in, sizing me up, modelling their wine collection for me every night. 'You should get a proper job, sort yourself out a bit,' he said before definitively hiring me. I had prompted this by saying, with a smile and a swig, that I still had plenty of time.

It is Daniel and Casey's last night. We're poking sticks in the expanding fire pit and pushing out our chests as we reign those logs in. They're on the trip of a lifetime, a real break from the mundanity of their lives. Constantly blogging back to home and just as constantly receiving feedback about how brave they are, what a courageous and wild thing it is they are doing, how they are such an inspiration and how *oh, I wish we could just drop it all and go off like that*. My brain glazes over slightly as I witness this again, the age-old motions of conversation. But they're nice, I like them. Such sweet smiles and the way they hold hands, grabbing in the half-dark like they've lost some favourite blanket for a moment, and then the physical relief that crumples through their bodies, drops their dia-

DISTANT HILLS

phragms and shoulders, as they locate their partner's edges once more.

They strongly urge I follow, that I work my notice and meet them up near Inverness for a tour of the highlands. It's almost tempting, *to follow*, to flow, to be told what is next. I could be their pet local, exchanging my anecdotes for their anecdotes, widening my range. But in the end I just can't do it. I let them go. We say night and I fog-walk back to my tent, struggle with the zip and my feet and most of my body before eventually aligning myself back inside. I hang the lamp and put my earplugs in and attempt to read but manage about a paragraph before sleep takes control of my eyes.

In the morning I awake to find them gone, just a rectangle of pale limp grass and a note inside my tent porch attached to an unwanted bottle of rosé wine. I drink a slug of water from a week-old plastic bottle and do my rounds of the pitches. Checked out, paid up—I draw a line through Casey and Daniel's names.

My nostalgia is hit hard almost immediately. The silence after a party. One head perfectly de-tuned so it lies in that furry realm between all music: white noise. The circling of the body. The trees remain where they are, but I am lying on that dream-hill again, in a pale pink dress I have never worn and never will. The hill is perfectly sculpted, billowing up, exhalation of ground. My shoes are white ballet pumps, and I spin. Me or the hill—opposing motions. Always this same image. In the sun (of course in the sun) and the wind. Arms out. Some kind of dizzying ideal. Draw a few birds in: the shape of *V*s, smiling cheeks. I told them to go without me. I wanted this.

IX.

ELSE IS HANGING around in my dreams. All I see is her face turned back to us as we wave and cheer her down the curving steps from Jaap's apartment. A facial expression I can't quite get to come into focus, smudged by repeated efforts to correct it. We're standing above, looking down, and her upturned face slides further and further out of focus. Neon sweatbands, bright pink lipstick, hair up in a ponytail so perfectly imperfect it should have been a logo for something. I want to lie down in the snow and have us throw balls of the weather at each other and start again from there.

I did write to my parents, mainly so that when I'm called to be accountable the balls are all already waiting in my court. There wasn't much to say; there's the past, which they know already; the present, which is largely a series of minor details either too irrelevant, too unprocessed, or too out-of-their-range-of-understanding to be worth mentioning; and the future, of which I either have no idea or they quite vocally disapprove. I signed off politely, warmly; they replied (deaths, births, marriages). We moved on.

I didn't write to Kathy. I didn't write to Aleksandar, though he wrote to me, checking up, checking in. I did write to a series of long-lost acquaintances I found as I first-letter-searched through my inbox, to see what might happen; nothing much did.

I've worked at the campsite for three months. Gained a bit of a countryside tan, fostered a little serenity. A comforting distance has settled in between me and the majority of passing events. I talk to Martha and Roy a few nights a week. Each Sunday night they sort of pity-cook for me to help supplement my diet of beans and cheese.

They bought the land ten years ago, when Martha suffered some heart problems and felt unable to continue work. Roy accepted a well-timed redundancy package and followed Martha's dreams. They relocated from Birmingham or somewhere close by enough that its syllables were immediately forgotten by me, and pitched up here. The summer help is usually quite a bit older or younger than me. Last year they had Roseanne, a lady in her late fifties with dry hair and large front teeth. She was from a neighbouring village, worked in the closed-for-summer school canteen. That made sense. The college students make sense, the international gap-year backpackers make sense; either trying to save money or provoke a little life experience for their future selves. But Roy and Martha don't know what to think of me, and I can't give them much in the way of context. We eat cottage pie and shepherd's pie and stew and hotpot and toad-in-the-hole and other things.

I tell them about my journeys, my childhood, some of the people I sometimes meet. They take sips of wine and nod and ask questions, but always looking on, lingering like two sets of impatient ellipses. *And? What's next?* they ask, because you're always supposed to know this, as they tell me about the three careers they've had each. *Maybe Iceland, maybe Canada, maybe Spain*, I say, *who knows*.

'What for? What's there?'

'Why not?'

'What are you looking for?'

'I just want to see.'

'What are you learning . . .'

'Loads of things . . .'

'. . . that you couldn't learn here?'

'. . . it'll all fall into place.'

'Not without a plan, it won't.'

'I can feel myself becoming better . . .'

'You need to know what you want to get out of all this.'

'. . . more rounded, more able, fuller, like I should be.'

'What does that even mean?'

'I just want to see.'

They tut at me like I've fallen off a slow-moving treadmill. The nights always end a little like this. We're all wined up and they're trying to look after me with their heavy hands full of experience and certainty, and I'm trying desperately not to be what I am but I can't and I've always been, and I guess that's my lot and this is how it will be. No sincere eyes, stern lines of questioning, wrinkled hands touching mine, or well-meaning suggestion has ever got me any closer. And no friendship or love affair or anything that might have blossomed into more than that has ever got me any closer.

DISTANT HILLS

There was once a man, or a boy, depending on the age of the person witnessing the scene, who might have got me up against the window frame of the world at least: although it's hard to know, and I sincerely doubt it. I think the only thing close to completing me was the enormity of his absence, that wide empty space, a full-fat longing for what wouldn't have worked anyway. I broke it off so it's impossible to know, and what is impossible to know is impossible to imagine and therefore completely impossible, doesn't exist.

He came to visit me in Poland. I hated the way he sang to himself as he walked across my apartment, hated the hair on his knuckles, broke it off via video-chat because I knew I would eventually, and that it might be harder further down the line. Might be in person, might involve tears. But I've said this before. And then I constructed him. Constructed our future lives together, positioned all else (Else, I miss you) against his long left side. Two things aligned; scrutinised for height, weight, width. Nothing in the future was right. The trouble with a fantasy is that it's hard to unremember it, hard to turn away. Like unseeing a death, unsaying a person's name.

He would have fixed my posture, made me a respectable member of modern life. We would have bought objects that almost matched but not quite, each item in each room of our city-centre flat attracting comments from our eclectic group of wholesome and innovative friends, each of whom had a unique talent, usually in the form of a novel-twist on a more traditional handicraft they had lovingly nurtured back from near extinction. We would have watched avant-garde films together, nestled under warm and stylish blankets, eating spoonful after spoonful of caramel-and-cookie-flavoured ice cream. It would have been alright. Next to him, I would have got myself on the right track, teased out a suitable form of professionalism, sold and promoted my services.

I would have happily pottered along, wearing jumpers, gazing at the periphery of the partner. Smiling at jokes as he tried to deliver them, drinking the beers he brought me in what he thought a reckless show of spontaneity, and standing politely toward the backs of concert halls drooling over quasi-wistful guitar-strung fluster songs. It would have been alright. I could have bought new shoes before the puddles caught up with them, got my hair cut before the ends were fried, got myself a cat without worrying about the price or where our next home would be. We would have lived under the blanket. Close.

But not too close. Eventually not even touching. I saw it all when he came to visit me, why I couldn't do it. When I looked at his knuckles. Fingernails I couldn't abide. Though I have that with everyone. Nothing wrong with them; just not mine. Couldn't have that face being in love with me for the rest of what would have been my complete and successful life. Couldn't save that one. Couldn't hug that one. Couldn't deal with another person's feet or ankles, the getting to know them. The being side by side.

His absence became an inflated balloon in a too-small room, beating as the air was pumped in; huge and grey like a minimalist art installation. And I, pressed against one of the walls, waiting for the gas to subside: so there would be enough space to carry on. A space into which walks the Lithuanian, into which walks Zlat and the dust-driven highways of outer Armenia. Into which walks Aleksandar and Kathy and Dasha, and Dean and Mona and Jaap and Wim and Anouk, and now Roy and now Martha and now Casey and now Dan. An absence quickly filled with Else and all the untouchable perfections I can now allow her to finally represent.

DISTANT HILLS

I live up against the side of an inflated balloon, begging to be embedded into the walls of a too-small room. A cage within a cage—there's nowhere to go and there's nothing but view.

X.

I STEP OFF the plane and breathe in. Standing on the wobbly staircase—uncertain metal. A place always has an initial smell; a perception of weather, humidity, sun, the breeze. My recently turned-on phone vibrates and I slide it out of my pocket, slow as the person before me. We're an impatient and anxious crowd—some coming, some returning home—*I'm here*, she says, *waiting in arrivals*.

Cardboard sign in her hand bearing my name. We're more than a decade estranged but her face still moves the same. A little less elastic, a little less like a crashing wave. We embrace, and already that's an answer. Answer enough, affirmation. A dive into the sea and finding out the water is warmer than you'd imagined. Comfortable. She's a travelling musician with a two-year-old child and she's living in Nova Scotia and I don't quite know why.

She puts me in her car and we drive. It's all fairly simple, as if I had got off a two-hour bus ride from one city to the next along. There's nothing approaching drama. Just two lives. Like staring out

DISTANT HILLS

of a train window and watching the railway lines merge and disperse; meanwhile there is throughout a certain smoothness to their running along. Like dancing; you pull out, you fold in, but always your hands are joined, the speed of one motion prompting another. She drives.

She tells me details as if I know the context, as if the context is also mine. About how the price of books has risen, how there's no courgettes in the local shops. Her son, Fazakerley, is with his dad in Antigonish for a few weeks, and we're headed to Wolfville to eat homemade pie and play a couple of gigs. The drive seems to last for hours, tree follows tree follows tree follows sign, broken up by an occasional coffee place or petrol station or chicken-heavy establishment, all made of corrugated panels. The clouds move predictably across the sky. The radio plays songs from the '90s. We sing all the words we know and blur our eyes.

It's very easy. She looks at me like we both know we're older now and that there's really something quite ridiculous about it all, us being allowed to carry on inside these grown-up bodies. Inside this vehicle.

'You never did learn to drive, did you?' she says.

'No.'

'Why?'

'Commitment issues.'

'Right.'

She cranks up the volume and I'm not sure I feel properly alive. The dullness of the landscape, the way that—other than a different popular choice of fonts, other than a few strange turns of phrase—this could be where we grew up, only on a larger scale. She looks six years old, twelve years old, eighteen; anything but this. This bandana-wearing, wide-hipped, hippy driver in her brown suede lace-ups. I pull my sunglasses over my eyes in the hope of something more extreme.

She's still got dreadlocks, so in her own way she too is denying what is becoming of us. Rows of herbs and pickles line her kitchen shelves. Crochet needles and scraps of knitting are left casually lying around. She feeds me kombucha; I drink it, it fizzes. Unimpressive. It is what it is. Tonight she's playing at the Irish bar. *I'm pally with the owner, I can get you a bit of work there*, she says. *Thanks, but I'm alright*, I reply.

We head down to the bar around eight o'clock, I even change my top for something with the sleeves off. I'm feeling somehow loose and playful. Like I want to do things the way they ought to be done, more lighthearted and less atmospheric-pressure deep-sea eject-button all at once. I change my socks as well, why not, and throw my scarf around my neck in an almost carefree fashion. I walk with my posture stretched upwards and with long slow breaths. The scene, the evening, the way the road signs are a little higher than I'm used to, the streets a little wider; the way the cars sport their bigger-than-I'm-used-to tyres. I want to take it all in and let it do something to me. Let these variations parade around inside me and alter what little substance lies therein.

She's strumming on strings and singing through chords and the lyrics are all about the greenery and a low-flying bird and the curves it makes and how like her son it flies and swoops and its motions are a miracle, both predictable and wild. The hairy man sat nearest to me with his thick rough thumbnails beats out a rhythm on the table with a thumb-side and through half-closed eyes. Relax-

DISTANT HILLS

ation hums all around, rises through the beer foam, through the gently bubbling stomachs and quiet in-mouth burps of confidently digesting and absorbing bodies. I stare at the lighting. Focus in on her hand or the way her eye stares at some memory or association rather than anything in the room. It's like everybody in here knows some same secret regarding the past and they're all sitting around swaying and stoking it. Swathes of smoke like ghosts brood upwards. I'm calm, sure. The atmosphere is catching. But none of this is mine.

No folk song belongs to me. No violin or fiddle or cello. No line or barn dance, no matter how many beers are revving up inside me. I can make the moves, laugh like an animal, but in the morning there remains a kind of emptiness, a high-definition vision of myself trying too hard. I try to think about a time when I am content, when I am nothing but myself. I see her there on stage, truly encompassing her own body. Reigning long inside her right to make music and to zone out her eyes in that way, to allow her voice to so publicly tremble. I look at the thick-thumbed man to my side, at his forlorn hair and misaligned outfit and how he slumps himself so firmly within that guise. And then down at myself. At my arm that might not even be enough of an arm. That, if questioned about it—*Why do you hold it like that? Those freckles, do you like them? Are you sure this is the best position for it, right here, on the table? Is that really how you raise a glass?*—I wouldn't be able to answer in any way that was at all convincing.

Side by side, stumbling up the pavementless hill, with the moon dubiously one-eyeing us and the stars flitting about their celestial business between withering cloud ends, she swings her strong arm around me and I'm sort of mothered, sort of guided, sort of stifled by this trophy from a past I have little to do with. Old school photos of fellow pupils with the eyes gouged out or the word *COW* scratched into their long-dropped cheekbones, evidence of ancient compasses. Yearbooks full of swear words, best friends for life, and crude allusions to what might one day approach sexual intercourse. That clutter and this arm are all I have left to confirm that particular decade ever happened. I'm on my knees and she's pulling me up and I'm laughing as usual because I didn't die yet and it can't be that bad and my whole life is in front of me, up this hill, somewhere between those next two lampposts and the possibilities are endless. She pulls me up and I'm all the properties of a spare single mattress, soft and pliable but inconvenient to move and not in the best form.

XI.

FAZAKERLEY IS ALL over me, leaping on, scurrying across mounds and nooks and prominent features. 'Eye,' he says, and pokes his finger in. 'Nostril.'

'Are you sure you'll be okay?' she asks, holding guitar, door handle, house key, raincoat.

I nod because there are tiny hands on my lips trying to gain access to the unknowable hole of my mouth. She smiles and winks and is simultaneously gone. Me and Fazakerley and the floor share a bag of dried apricots. I squeeze what is left of the moisture out after first bite with my tongue, the texture somehow repulsing me like certain bodies do after thick nights. A repulsion like preparing to pick up a handful of cold cooked spaghetti, rather than that of waking to the slivering sensation of what turns out to be a silverfish on your face in what would have been the middle of a dream. Fazakerley bites and spits, spits and bites.

After some attempts at conversation, Fazakerley dozes off next to me on the couch with his head in the crooks of my two bent knees. I take hold of the book I'd purposefully left within arm's reach and read the same page again and again. There is no such thing as progress.

Wolfville is a small town, with little over 3,500 people, although it feels much smaller. I frequent three bars, two cafes, two bookshops, and a handful of small shops that sell a clutch of plastic everything, all slightly more novel than the forms you find them in in other places. One of which has kindly employed me for the foreseeable future. I see the same fifty or sixty people, 20% of whom I talk to, whether that be while exchanging cash for services or after slugging my way through a third or fourth beer.

I open up easily when I know I have very little chance of remembering it. The divulged past flashes back at me in fragments, none of it very interesting, most of it so uncared for that its very reemergence often comes as a surprise. The thick-thumbed man got a barrage that first night, after my friend's set was finished, or maybe even earlier. Asked me where I was from, who I was with; received the whole shebang. It's hard to tell a story when you don't know the ending or what the point is; the angle, the moral. He proceeded to do the thing many thick-thumbed pub-goers do and fired his own back at me at the first available opportunity. So there we were, the one overlapping the other, crossing in time. Neither one really listening, making our same mistakes. He'd lived on a boat in Hamburg with a wife thirty years his junior, where they'd both worn eye patches and kept a dog and played at being pirates. He told me what he knew and I nodded while correcting with the vigour of youth; quoting passages from books I'd read when I was apparently coming of age. I told him what I knew while he shook

DISTANT HILLS

his head, full of wisdom and history and brittling opinions. Neither one of us really caring for the conversation, both role-playing for something better to come. For the one that counts.

The conversation ended with the clink of glass and the whiff of camaraderie and the feeling that we'd broken down some time-old barriers, crossed one more person off a list of those we felt alienated from and slung them on top of the must-keep-in-touch-with pile. Moved them over to the other side of the line. Avid collectors, the lot of us: making lists, completing levels, keeping scores.

Else told me once how she felt so sad that she was nothing, that everybody else she met had a *thing*, a sort of unique skill or defining characteristic. Else could speak four languages, once played in a semi-professional women's football team, and had grown up for six years of her teenage life in a remote village in South Africa.

The Lithuanian was a thing, the easy way neither of us actually cared much nor pretended to. At least in that carelessness there was an honesty, at least the way we shocked our elders was quick and undeceptive, didn't tie us to years and years of wishing it could have been other and subsequently lamenting our stolen youths. Things were simple, deconstructable, could be described, sketched, bottled, numbered, portioned out.

The child sleeps between my knees as if all adults are permanent structures. He breathes, I breathe; his faith almost convincing. She'll be a few hours more, I imagine, while staring past the pages of the book I'm holding and over to the fading, yellowing, organic print of the décor. Hooks stringed with onions, wild garlic, herbs whose names I don't know, and the guilt of ignorance that mocks me because of it. Details that look like they should collect more dust and mould than they do—every detail rustic, natural.

Leaves and petals brown and harden on shelves, are strewn around window frames and mirrors. The kind of leaves that have stepped out of society, nobly and successfully, and draped themselves around our attempts at civilisation, clawing it back. Twisting vines inch themselves between the close and frozen bonds of immediate relatives on family photographs.

Dead plants are more comfortable in our homes than we are. These children will expand to become us. Beds are the wrong length, mattresses don't conform to the contours of our side-long bodies. Backache is brought on by the mere act of sleeping, in animals so out of touch with themselves they don't even know how to repose. Articles telling one how to sit are carefully trimmed out of magazines and hoarded.

The door clicks open. I register the change in light through my still-closed eyelids and jump a little inside my body. She's home and turns on the tap, moves metal against metal, flicks the switch on the kettle. We haven't really spoken since I came.

'Are you awake?'

'I am now.'

'Oh.'

She begins to tiptoe away but I gesture her towards me. She pushes a buttock against my feet, which bend and make space in response.

'How was the gig?'

'Great, thanks. What is it you're really doing here?'

She looks at me. Huge don't-give-me-that look above a cup of fennel tea's steam. She doesn't mean anything to me. There is noth-

DISTANT HILLS

ing to say. Just years and years of proximity, grappling, and infighting. A string of memories flock to the surface and peck hard at a submerged wall. A fly lands on my thigh and I crush it with the smallest of movements, turn my palm over, rise to fetch a piece of tissue from the kitchen counter.

XII.

SHE'S LETTING ME stay for a few more months, on the condition that I babysit every Thursday and Friday evening and keep the kid with me all day Friday. She said perhaps we were very different people now, after all, perhaps there wasn't so much to discuss these days, but longevity in itself was no doubt an achievement worth holding onto. We try to spend Monday evenings together, just the three of us, but after Fazakerley goes to bed our conversations tend to deflate quickly into a handful of do-you-remember-whens and a few games of cards.

I replied to an advert looking for volunteers at some husky training centre deep in Alaska. They wrote back to me quickly enough to tell me I didn't get it. I thought about moving on to Saskatchewan or Manitoba, but after looking at the map for a while and only really meeting locals, students, and retired couples on holiday from Alberta, I figured all travel in rural Canada was pointless. I did meet a guy from Quebec—driving from somewhere I'd never heard of up to Labrador—we had a brief chat in the queue at the coffee place by my work, where both he and I noticed the other had an accent. Labrador. I thought about it. The chance to discover a really remote corner, get wild, connect with the earth. I could have asked him. Instead, I asked for a double-shot latte and waved goodbye as I was waiting to be asked whether I wanted it to drink in or to take away.

The plastic shop that has hired me was established in 1994. It mostly trades in multi-use containers of all shapes and sizes with a side line in offensive-humour socks and items made of tin. There are often three or four sets of people mulling around inside but rarely does business pick up to the extent that a crowd forms. The owner-manager is called Sandra, born and raised right here in Nova Scotia, and is forever telling me about all these inspirational women she has met over the years and how they have summoned their inner goddesses and made huge changes to their lives. She occasionally ventures down to Halifax where she attends watercolour classes, the results of which—mainly portraiture—she displays proudly round the store.

I don't have a car, so as far as possible I try to arrange for someone to take me home when I finish work. The house lies two kilometres uphill, and the road is straight and deep. I keep a schedule of who is where on which days and with what vehicle, and try and pull a few regular favours in. I bake brownies most Fazakerley-days in order to have something to offer the drivers, usually friends of friends of the handful of people I know.

Blaze is one of these drivers; he lives three kilometres uphill and so, he claims, dropping me off breaks up the journey. He has a dog;

it tried to bite me once when we bumped into each other on the walking trails up in the hills. Trained to protect him, Blaze said, from the moose, the bears, whatever else there may be. I must have smelt of Europe, he said. Said his dog hadn't never smelled anything out of Europe before. He apologised (Blaze) and the dog largely left me alone after that first instance. The occasional sniff. Me and Blaze go walking often when our shifts allow.

Blaze is quiet, which I like; no past on show. He points out minor anomalies in the trees as we slow-hike around. I've come to be able to distinguish many of them, to know one leaf from another, certain individualities of wear and tear. I anticipate what he's going to say as we approach a patch of moss or a mushroom shelf angling out from a wall of tree bark. Our conversations are more like pre-recorded radio shows rather than anything spontaneous or organic as these fields. It is hard to be with him for any length of time, but only in as much as it is hard to be anywhere, and it's nice, on this great mass of land, in this near empty region, not to have to try: Blaze just recites his descriptions in the same gentle manner that sea-foam has of shaving hairs from the coastline, and the objects of his attention, walk by walk, also become the objects of mine.

In Canada I feel the universe expanding—hardware stores travelling hundreds of miles an hour in opposing directions, villages spreading apart, mass-produced plants replicating as the asphalt is laid on mass-produced roads. Perhaps I could stay in a place like Wolfville, because a place like Wolfville convinces me there is no place else near enough to go.

Blaze takes my hand. In the world-lined path through the hills that give the rolling mist a place to be watched from, he takes it and

DISTANT HILLS

sort of travels around it with his double-sided finger-laced arms. Tree limbs trail and conquer, shield and lunge and swerve. Blaze takes his eyes and presents them to me on the cushion of an upturned palm. *It's a long way to go*, he says, and projects us both mushroom-ward into the side of a mound of earth.

Pillows of moss balance each other like air escaping and re-entering interconnected yet sealed compartments. The moment persists. Volcanoes erupt underwater, sending smooth liquid metal upwards in domes. Time slows, geology becomes a thing that can be seen and known. Strangler fingers curl around my desperately seeking stem that is doing the best it can given the circumstances into which it has been grown.

Blaze takes my hand and my eyes and the present and sort of travels around them, seeing which way he should go. He plucks the sun off its microphone stand and angles the light around. Absolutely nothing matters. There is not one thing in the world I would request to be saved in the event that demand were made of me. Lips touch like land masses moving uneventfully toward each other. Mountain ranges sprout up as they were bound to, at some point, eventually. Continents are consequently embittered and divided. Generation after generation, certain animals find their rafts and escape to terrain as yet unknown.

Walking back, the kilometres feel like miles and my hand remains very much possessed. We arrive at Blaze's. He invites me inside. I decline. Not wanting to press the matter, he relinquishes that hand of mine, and I take the last kilometre alone.

I tell Fazakerley about the eagles, about the orange glow through the permeable near-canopy of pines. I empty my pockets of the small rocks and stones I bring back for him every time I go out walking in the hills of Nova Scotia and he rushes to place them on the shelf where his collection of that sort of thing goes.

XIII.

AT THE PLASTIC shop, Sandra is going through a divorce; it's the age-old battle of the assets. Who earned what and who raised who and what was each thing worth? One person's time in the boxing ring against another; care vs. capital; creating well-rounded and self-aware individuals vs. keeping the prices down. Sandra had kept the plastic shop up and running and her soon-to-be-ex-husband had largely stayed home with the twins while they were small. He'd lost his job around the same time she'd become pregnant and they had both decided this was the best way round: that looking after the babies would warm his heart and keep his esteem bubbling over far more than harvest after harvest of fruitless job search. Years out of work turned into more years out of work and now Sandra doesn't want to give him half the house.

Sandra's portraits line the shop rafters. New ones keep coming, though every month with a new harshness; reddened eyes, lips slightly pursed. Sandra's hands tremble, drops of dried-up watercolour dot the shop floor.

Blaze picks me up after closing time. I'm a bit behind as Sandra is crying in the stock room and I have a lot of plastic buckets I need to take down from right above where she is sitting; however I don't want to be the one to go over there and mollify all that emotion. Instead, I'm brushing up the dead flies and half-demolished spider webs that incongruously scatter themselves around, as the sun dips its tip into the surface of the Minas Basin and blurs fireball-yellow to a water-soaked orangey-brown.

'Are you ready?'

'I can't. Can't you hear her? Go and say something.'

'Me?'

'You live here.'

'*You* live here!'

'No I don't, not like you do. Go on, please, it's been at least forty minutes. She's getting a divorce.'

'Are you serious? You work with her. Like, every day.'

'I can't.'

'Why not?'

'I can't.'

'What do you need to do? Why are *you* crying?'

'Plastic buckets.'

'Is it important? Can it wait? What time are you in work tomorrow? Do you need a lift? I can drive you in a little early if you like.'

I nod. I nod to everything.

'Will she notice if we just go?'

I eyebrow my way through a quick range of emotions—distaste, concern, resignation—until we leave anyway. I close the door gently, having twirled through the ajarness of it gently; I rotate and

DISTANT HILLS

return-rotate the handle of it gently, gently watch the lock become a dark rectangle across the thinness of the light-filled line of imperfection between door and frame. I look Blaze in his quiet eyes and press my waist against his quiet outstretched palms.

It's not that I don't care about Sandra. I do. I care about everybody.

'Do you want to come back to mine for a while?' Blaze asks.

'Why not,' I reply.

Overdue dishes, dog hairs. Bare bulbs and curtains once belonging to a now-abandoned mother somewhere. We watch a movie on the low couch, curled into each other, our bodies repeating; the couch sagging like city steps ground down. We are in the groove and I point this out and Blaze laughs and, more than that, he smiles. I feel his fingers squeezing my shoulder, involuntary tightenings and my involuntary attention toward them. The film bearing witness to the seconds elapsing until again that pressing, pressure, presence. There is this closest thing and then there is closer still. One can always exaggerate. The rope is tied, but its ends can always be pulled at a little more. A little more air in the tyre. A screw screwed for one more quarter turn. A balloon blown. Nothing is ever complete. And again that pressing. One more turn.

The movie moves and we hold faster, bearing witness to the sluggish script elapsing. Grasping this opposite body we have decided just now to adore. 'Do you want to stay?' he says. (*Forever*, I think). 'Sure.' Bed springs and night hours and full sets of clothes and arms taking hold and grey curls of hair. Glasses lie pathetically on the bare wooden table, its wooden lining peeling away to reveal more wood beneath. A thinner body than mine yet I hold it like I might be the weaker object. Faces in chests, faces in backs. Hot arms that seem to mean something as their weight is felt on responsive sides. Sleep that enjoys breaking. Smells that enjoy being secretly caught. Intermittent eye contact, because that's what we're really afraid of: pupils asking who we are. Are we really able to sleep together? Maybe, if we both turn to the outside. My hands travelling down every one of his sleeping fingers and examining the shape of every crease and every knuckle and every nail. There is history in here somewhere, in this solid body. Bed covers keeping the rest of reality at a utilitarian distance. This cave, this tent, this den we are hiding in. The noise of his next-to-me-nowhere-else nose. His face the shape of a shield and his brain held up like a fist behind it. In the dark a dimple at the side of another smile; how, as it forms, it sucks away the night's excess air.

Talking so fast and strong, all hand gestures and opinions we don't really feel as much as we want to appear to be feeling, desiring all the while to be true and passionate to the cores. A conversation severed by the length of sleep, now picked up again as if the seven-second rule was still six and a half seconds from applying. Legs that slide between legs and to and back from the toilet and out and again into a raw-sprung bed. Documentaries, directors, cinematography, direction. Truth vs. The Contrived, the pleasure of the mammoth task, seeing a distant goal and giving it presence, pushing a boat up a hill, small towns and big imaginations, everything I never did, until we did and did and did and we keep on defining our continuation with our fraught and hopeful mouths. Elbows, shins, please believe me, I'll stay here, I promise, I'll stay forever, we'll weave in and out of each other like two halves of a double-helix, complicated proteins, you'll be my chapel, I'll be your steeple. I can't fall asleep with your hand under my head, under my neck, but I do it anyway because I want to be held in place. To be sure. The hours pass and I'm here and I'm here and I'm here and the dark air conflates on my endless shape, as I lie awake, true and symmetric, inside myself. I touch your leg. I breathe in. Blink. Exhale.

A month, two months, three. Is this what I want? Is this what I've always wanted? Once a fortnight I go to the cinema to watch the latest release in this town. There isn't much to choose from so I (we—me and Blaze—it's almost the same thing) watch everything, soak it all in. Harrison Ford, Meryl Streep, they're all at it, starring in things. Blaze puts his arm around the back of my shoulders and we look exactly like any one of the adverts for Wolfville's coming-soon films. Lights, trailers, parental guidance (if you're lucky), action. Running time. Critic's ratings. The credits roll.

Three months, four months, five. Wolfville. The treeline. The north-side of hills. Man-made tracks. 4x4s. Rabbits landing with their rear legs fore and their forelegs rear and inside. I could have died before this point many times. My life, anyone's, is a series of near misses; rocks cascading, anvils falling, the ground crumbling away behind us and to our sides. Stone walls change colour, the wildlife and the vegetation alters, time-zones are shaken up. Emails remain the only constant, with their certainty of font and line of questioning: *How's it going? What have you been up to? When are you coming home?*

If you pay enough attention to the tracks in the hills eventually you see one of three things: a commute, an escape, or a chase.

Blaze puts me on, takes me off, clothes me, holds me. It's the weekend, any, and we drive forever to the big city, Halifax, and we're staying in a hotel and enjoying ourselves. Having an adventure, an experience. We're eating curry on the third floor of a great big cube of metal with restaurants and massage parlours and a gym inside. The restaurant is kitted out to look as if it isn't situated on the third floor of a metal cube, and we take starters, poppadoms, lassi, the lot. We take it and savour or devour, but rarely anything in between.

Blaze looks at me like he's about to speak. A waiter passes. Blaze orders another drink.

Sleeping with Blaze in the hotel room is novel for a moment. It feels sort of special and we bought a bottle of Prosecco and drank nearly most of it, but after maybe twenty minutes I'm just sleeping with Blaze the same as anywhere, except I'm here. Except here I'm worried I'm not making the most of it, in a way I wouldn't be worried at his house or in a regular old copse littered with folded cans of lager, or in a storage room with wall-to-wall plastic-bucket lined shelves. I don't deserve these bedsheet folds.

The hotel room looks out over the promenade that leads to the immigration museum. We take pasta for lunch in an elaborate eatery. My dish is so layered in parmesan that I start to feel decadent, a feeling that filters my entire surroundings in a simple instant, landing just behind the eyelids and fusing flawlessly with my previous state of mind. Blaze is disappointed by the food, I can tell, but he doesn't want to ruin it so he just sits there chomping on his

DISTANT HILLS

meatballs and depositing his hidden sulk into his second glass of lunchtime wine. The immigration museum tells us about who came and went and when and what for and how tragically some of them died. We leave the museum and stand next to each other staring at the water for quite a long time. I try to imagine distance but the concept is too far spoiled. We are at the wrong angle to see the sun go down so we wait for the clouds to darken a little, look at our watches, and decide we should probably go home.

XIV.

I HAVE MOVED in to Blaze's. It seemed easier. It is. Easier than rooting around the bottom of a handbag for a toothbrush and plucking out bag crumbs from between the flattening bristles. Easier than creeping through a house that isn't mine through rooms I don't feel comfortable illuminating at certain hours of the day or night, toward the one room I have some kind of power over but which I'm only ever sleeping on the surface of, only ever dreaming of, only ever imagining hanging pictures on the walls of, while fantasizing about winding the place tightly around the prosaic skin of my unhoused form.

I still go and look after Fazakerley every week; she has no problem with that. Only with my bringing Wolfville home.

When we were children we did everything together, either just before or just after one another, a sort of glitch-heavy coupling of mirrors bouncing back and forth like sticking a just-copied photocopy back in a photocopier and then sticking that new photocopy back in the photocopier to be photocopied again, and so on. It should come as no surprise then when the original image is unidentifiable and the resultant pixelated dots don't want to hang out together anymore, each blaming the other for their long-unrecognisable rendering.

Still, you try and keep it meaningful. You never know how things are going to appear when you look back at them from afar. Nobody wants to be the bad guy until they are and they start trying to convince themselves this was what they always meant to happen. She's the same, it's more or less the same, when we talk, the ups and downs of tones and arms; the laughter comes and it's real enough. But something lies between us like a great wall of polystyrene absorbing sound, like the last time I saw my father and I just stood there and noticed I didn't care at all, what was said, what was meant, what went before, and I just took my pint and said thanks and sat down.

You never know. So we keep talking. I'm not sure which one of us wants it less, which one of us wants it more. One thing I am sure of is that it is always a battle, there's always something inside it, words loaded with all the things words used to mean and all the things we thought they might mean by the time we got to wherever it is we currently are. And every chat about her music career or how things are at work or with Sandra or my health or how I shouldn't be feeding Fazakerley this or that or something else, it's all worth so much more than we give it credit for. But no one says it, no one ever says it.

She won't talk about Blaze. She pulls all the jars of her pickle selection closer to the front of the shelf, turns them round so all the labels are pointing out. I tell her it's going well, that haha who could have imagined we'd both end up here, in Wolfville, her with a son and me with a mechanic, and all that stuff with her mum, don't worry, I never told anyone, just in case she was wondering, because who would I tell? What did it matter? Let bygones be bygones, that's what I say. And while we are on the subject, it's cool about that fight we had in the train station that time, the really nasty one, and about that time she pushed me into the road (she was drunk, it wasn't intentional, we all were), and I've done my share too, I know, screamed and said things I didn't mean, even though I perhaps never said them with quite the same venom as she. But we overcame all that, eh, like sisters we are, we've been through some things, adventures, haven't we, and I'm sorry to be moving out, although I'm sure you'll appreciate getting your own space back, finally, I know I said just a few weeks, and here we are, so many months down the line, almost a year, and it doesn't look like I'm going anywhere any time soon now, hah. She pulls all the jars of her pickle selection closer to the front of the shelf and turns them round so all the labels are pointing out.

There is so much downtime.

XV.

SHE DOESN'T LIVE here anymore. And I'm somehow in her wake, as if her absence has left me even more displaced. She wasn't Wolfville and she wasn't me, Fazakerley wasn't mine and I didn't want him to be, but children are useful markers of permanence, of progress—without doing anything, you succeed simply by being alive over the breakneck speed of their life. They remember you, in the short-term, which to them is forever, and so to you it becomes a kind of forever, too. And when they go it's a death, like my shock when I saw a friend's kitten again after several years and he was limping and enormous and blind. You can leave adults for years and when you rejoin them it's pretty much the same—thinner, hairier, new coat, hair dye—but this, this is new, this is a real ending; he won't remember me. I'm a dream, a double-take, a historical event. Not quite a stranger, but not much more than the recognition of a colour, the sky being blue, grass being green, things as they are supposed to be. His mother shows him an apple and he says, yeah, that's what I thought. Yet, for me, that next meeting (if it comes) will be like seeing an apple that can fly. Like fists against a one-way mirror. Like screaming the name of a long-lost love as they hunker down into the noise of their headphones, eyes only for the oncoming traffic, and cycle away.

She sold the house to a new-age mother in her sixties and her son, who was also called Wolf. They stripped the walls and hung fake Persian rugs from wall to ceiling; other than that small amendment and the exchange of one incense smell for another, the transition was seamless, a perfect relay. Wolf is troubled and thin, sombre and wise; always staring off into the distance even when the viewable distance is not so very far away. He glares through walls, his gaze reaches America, Ireland, Vancouver, the icy poles.

I'm here with Blaze but without what might have been the reason I came. We didn't speak about it, she slipped out quietly. Tripped off to Saskatoon with her guitar and her van and her boy. The lengths of the roads here. I thought about discovering the country, the continent—made it to Quebec and came back again having just run a marathon in my brain. No. This world is too big for me. Halifax was the other end of the earth, and the two friends we made there, who I occasionally write to (letters, as is fitting with the scale), I doubt I will ever see again. I can't imagine travelling far enough to reach anyone. Can't imagine the stamina. And even if I did make it, the thought of the return journey would be too much to contain.

The hardware store is two hours' drive away. The effort it took to put up a shelf and buy a new coffee table. Sometimes you travel to the shop and don't find what you need, or you're unsure, you don't want to jump straight in, so you come back empty-handed, weary with the knowledge you'll have to do it all over again. We usually go

DISTANT HILLS

together, Blaze and I, but it doesn't help relieve the burden, only leaves us delicate and apologetic, ashamed at our selfishness, at our wasting such huge chunks of the other's life. I hold his hand, grateful, in the back of Sandra's car as she drives us there. One link in a chain. I am hanging from a rope-swing hanging from a tree in the pouring rain.

She has gone. The deforestation continues. Don't look back. I hold Blaze's hand tight. I swing to Sandra, high-five, and back again. It will be alright.

We sleep with the curtains open to make the most of the available light. I would rather sleep in the world than in a room; I want connection. I want all my movements to be as subtle as installing Persian rugs behind a pickle collection on a rural shelf. I want to put my hand out and touch dusk, birdsong, sleet, perfume. I want to hear an owl or the rain and not to feel so very far away. I want a smooth line, I want to hear the sun rise, I want to wake and know what time it is at all junctions of the night and to then decide. I see Blaze's face in the moonlight and that feels right, the right way to see it, with the moon on his cheek instead of this curtain-clothed darkness we foster and this unrelenting electrical light.

She's gone; they're all gone. Memories become maybes, and I, my hand, my arm, lies round the certainty of Blaze. The hairs around his navel, that's where I stay; the forestry there soft and uniform, undemanding yet persistent like life colonising newly formed land. My hand like a cloud crossing terrain: spider-loose and interested only in absorption. I love him most at night, when we are nothing other than bodies paused between better days.

XVI.

BLAZE ARRIVES HOME with two pizzas, two chocolate bars and two bottles of beer. Trying to hold it all behind his back and failing. The failure becomes part of the act; the treats tumble to the ground and he alongside. I get to choose first, from each of the three categories. Blaze's real skill lies in the selection process, in my wanting everything he has on display.

We eat and hold and look and talk. It is very uneventful yet the way the window catches the light, the angle of the corners of the rooms—oblique, not quite charming. His family are coming over in the late afternoon, driving in from their house next to nothing very much on the other side of town. His mother coughs for most of the evening; I find it hard to concentrate, to present myself appropriately. Midway through a lot of my stories she breaks out into a cough and I feel the anger rising up inside my chest, my eyes pressing a little harder against the inside-front of my head. I try but my personality is not shining through. I lose the impact of a lot of my

DISTANT HILLS

tales. I hear it coming, the cough. I hear the rattling down at the back of the throat and I just don't see any point in going any deeper into what I am trying to say. I lose confidence in my own ability to compel, to sustain anything, and abate. My hands limpen and my gaze trails the walls like a fat slug at sun-up hearing the approach of human footfall down the staircase and looking for a way to escape.

The father grunts and scoffs and smiles and puts his big old hand on my arm, my knee, the surfaces of a lot of Blaze's nearby objects. He is a receiver. He asks no questions. There is no attempt at understanding; the best I can hope for is acceptance, recognition. And something about the sponginess of Blaze's father, something about the way all information is lost as it hits him and no sound escapes, makes me want to keep talking. I try telling him about my childhood, my parents, my siblings, the things I once thought I wanted, how I expected it would turn out, how it was expected I would turn out. All in a couple of hours, over some locally sourced salmon and some bottles of chilled white wine. There is very little reaction. He talks about boats and immigration and the Irish and the people who toiled this land before they were displaced. I say *yes but* or *that reminds me of* or *you remember how I just told you about*, but history is history and I am not enough of a part of it yet; I am still becoming known, still being welcomed into the grand old fold. Blaze watches me, brings his mother water, tops up glasses, pats his dog.

I stay sat next to the father; he spurs me on. I want to break through and be seen or heard. I want to stand on the table and demand that the coughing stops, demand that the epoch-soaked glaze be wiped from the father's overcast eyeballs, and demand that that fucking dog be taken outside. I love Blaze, I do, but how I have ended up with a dog in my life again, I have no idea. I want to clap my hands once, no reverberation, like hitting the white ball so it hits the aimed-for ball but doesn't itself move. I want precision, I want an audience, and I want to calmly, firmly state my preference. I want you, mother- and father-Blaze, I've been waiting. I have come so far. I don't see my family, I don't see my friends. I've been waiting for you, for this, for just this moment. And, so, this is it? This is all you are?

Blaze is holding a hand over my brow and a cloth over my hand. He looks into my eyes with two of the widest and most open doors I think I have ever seen. I try and grab a handle with my unclothed hand but he catches it, sets it down again. I've had a bit too much wine, his mum and dad have gone to bed. Turns out I started playing tunes I liked, turning up the volume—anything to muffle the coughing—tried to get his parents and him to sing. He explains to me gently that his parents aren't angry or even annoyed, just surprised and a little taken aback by my forcefulness. They are nearly eighty, he reminds me, and not used to their acquaintances jumping up on chairs and trying to persuade them to stand against their will.

I hear his mother hacking in the bathroom upstairs. I ask how long I was out for. He says not too long, it's not too late, that I went quiet and then it started to rain. That I snapped out of it, devoured the half bottle of wine that was sitting on the floor beside me, and seemed to come back to life again.

He asks if I want to go for a walk and we do. It's the tail-end of dusk and we do a loop to the streetlamp at the corner of the lane and back, as ever two of the only pedestrians on the road. Blaze

DISTANT HILLS

has left the dog at home, and I hear the swooping and fluttering of the bats, I hear the distant tide slapping the walls of the bay below.

'My parents are taking the dog,' he says.

'Oh?'

'Yep. Tomorrow.'

'Why? Was it something I . . .'

'They want to, they love that dog. You didn't mention it.'

The highest tides in the world are down there, they say, but I've hardly even noticed. Second largest whirlpool in the Western Hemisphere, but all I see are waves. It rains when we go there and a fat mist sags inside the coves. I walk in the brown sand, placing my feet with what looks like purpose, listening to the sensation of touching ground, of having the ground give way. Blaze has my arm in his hand, keeping pace. The wind blows our looser sections to their moderate extreme positions: hair, toggles, laces. My rain trousers slap my calves like insistent useless sails, genetic dead-ends, stalemates.

'I like you,' Blaze says.

'I had noticed something, yeah.'

'I mean really.'

'I'm looking for fossils, Blaze. Wanna quit rubbing it in and help me a little . . .'

'I mean really.'

'. . . pull your weight . . .'

'I want you to stay here with me.'

'On the beach?'

'In Wolfville.'

'Come on, Blaze, it's not every day we come down to the beach to seek out remnants of former worlds . . .'

'It could be.'

'We've got to make the most of these precious—'

'Will you marry me?'

XVII.

I DIDN'T FIND any fossils on the beach that day. Just my luck. Like how I never found any amber on the beaches in the north of Poland no matter how many times I tried. My friend Wojtek always would; he'd strut back over to me, us, whoever, with his head low and his arms wavering by his sides. And we knew. That fake modesty, the joyous pantomime of his crouched neck, of his fake-shuffling feet that were really hidden strides. We knew.

I have a small green jewellery container I think once belonged to my mother on a shelf or probably in a box somewhere, where I keep all the morsels Wojtek gave me. I had. And I don't remember if it was hers. What does it matter. I seem to remember that it was about to be thrown away, that I saved it. The lid is broken. Was. Is. I don't know.

The most fossils I ever saw in the wild was on a beach out by The Burren in West Ireland. Rocks like oil slicks, huge black slabs leaking into the water. Once your eye latched onto a first fossil, they turned up wherever you sent your gaze. Tiny, white, once-trying spirals. Helpless coils clinging tightly to their central promenade. I love walking on rocks, feeling my ineffective feet ape their interrupted shape. I love standing at the cliff edge and imagining that sea monsters have taken the rest of the world away. A warm wind blowing landward, like the arm of some great protector, urging me to go back the way I came.

In Mongolia I stood in the eye of a twister. I was in the desert, days away from anything that was not either desert or something very similar to desert. It was like walking through a waterfall. You close your eyes and wait for the rush, wait for the worst to be over. You step through, come out the other side. Only, with a twister, the other side is the middle and at some point you have to do it again, reclose your eyes.

I've booked a flight to Europe. Last night at work I told Sandra everything. How melodramatic Blaze was and how he had to go and ruin a precious thing by making it so much more serious. Trying to take me under his wing. Trying to keep me and make me a part of him. Of Wolfville. I couldn't stay here, in a place this small, on a landmass so big. I'm from Europe; continent of countries you can hop like bars, land of multinational week-long sightseeing cruises. You're in the sea, you're in Barcelona, you're back in the sea, you're in Rome. Not my idea of a holiday, but I feel safe knowing it's a thing. That I can comprehend the size of my environment. Canada is like being thrown out of an orbiting spaceship into the head-crushing endless nothing of eternal night. I couldn't stay here. Here I'm an ant who'll never make it to the end of the garden. I can read all about the fence in the monthly Canadian fence magazine when the big trucks come in, sure, but I'll never see it. I don't want to live in a land whose edges can't fit into my dreams.

Sandra shushed me a while and wiped my tears with her dust-coated apron then with the cloth she had just used to wipe the tills. She asked if Blaze knew how I was feeling, asked if I wanted to stay at hers again tonight. I said he didn't. I said I did. I have to tell him, I know I have to tell him. My flight leaves in a few days, a week, around then. There's still time.

I guess Blaze figured out I'm not marrying him, or that I don't seem to want to be marrying him. I would say I made it fairly obvious I won't be marrying him any time soon. I didn't look up, didn't answer. Just kept walking. I really wanted to find a fossil: a souvenir to make the coming worthwhile. I didn't know what to say. What can you say? Does anyone ever say no? They must. But then what? A list of reasons? A not-being-in-the-mood-for-it? A don't-believe-in-it? An I-don't-love-you? Not that. Never that. An I-don't know-how-to-love-anything?

Poor Blaze. I thought maybe I did love him, but you have to trust your instinct. My gut reaction was *fuck no, get me out of here*. And the gut always wins.

I remember seeing that twister shaking about in the van's windscreen. We started clapping our hands against things—backs of chairs, reusable water bottles, each other—saying *get out, get out, get out, let's go look at it, come on*. Four of us and the driver, Oggi, tumbled out of the van and were immediately subdued. Freeze frame. The twister continued its scatty dancing through and around our body-rimmed open mouths, and there we stood, mid-pose, mid-step, arms up and out, or paused midway to grabbing for our cameras. My vision vignetted around the flighty dust tube. In the same second of un-pause we all lunged at it, sand in our eyes, in our teeth, battering our cheeks, arms, areas of exposed scar tissue, our too-thin clothes. It was painful in the way getting an entire side of your body tattooed in the same second must be painful, but we'd never seen such a thing before.

It was the only real event in seven days of relentless driving. The day before, there had been a sheep on what Oggi called the road.

I think maybe I've been Blaze's only event for a long time.

When I lived in Serbia I was seeing a divorcee for a while. It was a small town, not much in the way of transient inhabitants. Me and a couple of others. An older guy called John whose only attachment to anywhere seemed to be his forever-almost-dying mother who had him duty-bound into a kind of annual rhythm of visitations that thus forced upon him a place to reluctantly call home; and a half-Finnish girl called Lucia who learnt Chinese from CDs in her rental room late at night and never came out when you invited her but always complained of being alone.

The divorcee was funny. Too funny. I got the feeling he was trying with everything he had left to impress me, to be entertaining enough, to define himself via the level of the glint in my eyes. It was that 'left' that troubled me. Like he was all used up, life essence in rapid depletion, health bar on the border of orange to red. I kept hearing the game-over music start up, then he'd tell a joke or eat an apple and kick his heels and we'd stomp off down the road, until I wondered if I had imagined the sound.

DISTANT HILLS

One evening, in my rental room, he removed his T-shirt. He was wearing an off-white vest underneath. I was maybe twenty-three years old and I don't think I'd ever seen a vest on a living person before. Possibly at a fancy-dress party somewhere, but never in anyone's actual life. There was what seemed to be a tea stain a little way beneath one of the nipples. The divorcee's usually booming half-American voice was suddenly reduced to a spiky whisper, like a sea anemone in a school photograph who's just realised he's the only one hilariously displaying his insides—red-raw and trying to collect it all back in again. He lay on top of me and I had to put my hands on the vest and kiss the vest and laugh at the jokes the vest was making. Because I couldn't tell him that I couldn't look at him now (though I couldn't), and I couldn't tell him why (though I knew). I still remember the feel of it, flimsy and rough, like an old sack. I drank red wine. Got through the evening. I was present, I was funny and responsive and kind, but also I was not. I was also inside my own head screaming VEST VEST VEST and looking at my watch and pushing myself brusquely forward with a palm right in the centre of my back, and tutting and nudging all the other parts of me that lived in there and pointing at my performance and doing stage whispers and rolling my eyes.

I don't want anyone to need me, it makes me nauseous, and this isn't the first time. That vest told me that nobody else had seen him this close to naked since the wife who had left him, and who he still occasionally mentioned in bitter tones; and that meant that either no one wanted him or there was nobody new in this town to want him, or he hadn't tried. And I got the impression that he tried. All this added up to the likelihood that I was the first one, the only hope in a town where everyone was related, departed, or married already. I couldn't be a part of that.

He stood outside my apartment regularly for weeks after that night. I'd get texts saying, *Why aren't you returning my calls?* Or *I can see you at your computer by the window.* Or *Come outside.* I wasn't a bold enough person to tell him the vest had killed his disguise.

My favourite ice cream as a child was a tongue-shaped yellow with a marbling of green and purple and pink running through it. The taste was incredible: rainbow flavoured; pure joy. One day I read the packaging before I opened it: *toffee-flavoured*. I didn't believe it. How could that unfathomable taste be simply 'toffee'? I ate the lolly. It was toffee. Disappointingly toffee. I never bought one again; and whenever my 'favourite ice cream' was bought for me by attentive adults I feigned a smile and felt the grenade of shame drop in my insides.

I have to go and see Blaze. All my stuff is still there. Only now Blaze isn't Blaze. It's as if someone's sucked all his vitality out and he's just some dried-out husk of a shape. I imagine walking along the hillsides with him arm in arm and I feel sick. I imagine sitting next to him in the cinema, shoulders touching, catching glances, and I also feel sick. I imagine flirting with his parents, asking them deep and personal retrospective questions and I feel embarrassed and undignified. I feel tricked, and ashamed at my ability to be so. I imagine his hand touching mine, I imagine his body touching mine. Goosebumps form in lines as my mantle sends tectonic shudders down my spine.

XVIII.

ON THE PLANE I peel back the foil sealing the largest of my metallic economy-class dishes and the steam quickly knocks out what might have been tears forming in my eyes. I let it. I leave my eyes there, blinking in the too-hot vapour. The woman to my left knocks my plastic cup off my plastic table while rooting around for something in her black leather, faux-leather, something-skin handbag. Apologises. Tries to reach to the ground to put it back. Can't. I tell her not to worry and lean over, stretching my arm down through the narrow gap between the two tables. Up to the shoulder in grey plastic I root around with my hand on the floor. Foot, foot, bag, foot again, got it.

'I've got it,' I say.

'Oh good. I *am* sorry. Butterfingers. Or elbows, I should rather say. It was my elbow, after all. Anyway, I do apologise.'

'It's fine.'

'I'm Harriet.'

'Hi.'

'Hello. I'm sorry, I'm just trying to find my . . . bloody handbags . . . never-ending world of . . .'

She knocks the cup off again.

'Oh! Sweetheart!'

'Really, it's fine.'

The plane trembles. I pull the window-blind up half way and look at the tapering orange belt connecting the earth to the sky. A loose curtain-hook coupling, one tug and it all tears away. Sun like a buckle, sinking in to the blue folds of skin around the waist of the distance. We are ripped from the universe as easily as pulling a piece of paper from a ring-bound notebook, left staring at our frayed and scattered margins, pretending we prefer it this way. Harriet squeezes a cloud of lime into her tonic-laced gin. Winks at me, adjusts her earphones, raises her plastic glass and doffs it a little, drinks. I turn back to the choices on my screen.

I am dreaming about being pursued. I have fought my way out of an altercation. A man's head in the toilet bowl and I have flushed the handle, the head has turned to metal and torn away. This wasn't what I intended but I had to be saved. I hold it up, an ornamental silver skull, and consider the consequences of the body that has just fallen to the tiled floor. There is someone standing in silence next to me because there is always at least one witness, either egging you on or tagging along. Then there is the knowledge of having buried the body, of having completed a job and having barely escaped.

The rest of the dream involves my everyday carrying on, routine tasks and persistent checking of newspapers. In this part of the dream, long and static, I am always pursued. It is always possible to get caught. It is easier to get caught than to explain. I watch somebody else getting caught and know it could be me at any moment. I wake with the moment of headless death repeating in my mind and Harriet's bird-claw fingers coiled around my porous hand.

'Are you okay, love? Nervous?'

The belt at the horizon is wide and white and rising up to delete the night. I blink and stare out across the cloud bed, drink an offered coffee, and rub the flecks of crust from my high-up eyes.

The plane touches down in Dusseldorf airport and I have given myself a week to decide. Cheeks are pulled back toward ears as the ending signifies the speed of the ride. I say bye to Harriet. Wonderful, settled Harriet whose life was summarised and stylised over the course of two gins and a watered-down white wine. She gave me her email address and invited me over for Christmas next year. Since her husband died and her daughters emigrated to Switzerland and Australia, she doesn't really have many plans that time of year, she tells me, applying a layer of fox-ochre lipstick in the darkness of her sleeping in-flight screen. Of course, she does go to Switzerland most years, but when there is another alternative it's good to mix things up a bit. She kisses me on the cheek and is gone.

I'm sitting on a bench facing the river, looking out across what seems to be a nice day coming on. I have a cheese-and-salad-filled baguette occupying my mouth and hands. My backpack is tucked between my two feet, their sides pressing against its, each making sure the other is still there: a buddy-scheme for one. My ankles are open to the breeze. I didn't see Blaze. I left Sandra with enveloped notes to pass along. Sometimes there is no point staying to fix what you have recently broken. You can see the pieces; and you can either try to collect them all up from the corners of the room, taping or gluing them back into what seems to be the correct position, finally looking at your patchwork, earthenware museum-piece result, the silence and scars of which will haunt you forever; or you can sandblast the uneven surface smooth and start again.

I'm sitting on a bench facing a wide river, pigeons gathering around my feet because I have bread and they don't know me at all.

XIX.

ALEKSANDAR IS LIVING in Frankfurt with his boyfriend Fab. I take the train over to meet him because in Europe anything is possible, space can be crossed, distance is your friend. We are having lunch in an ex-squat turned vegan diner and it is so good to see Aleksandar's face, to see his detail and how time has rubbed its shape across it. The features soften, the pencil lines continue to be drawn in. The whole picture becoming darker, sadder, yet at the same time geological, important.

Fab goes to the toilet and Aleksandar quickly fumbles an apology for being shit when Else died and saying it was too heavy and he didn't really know her very well, let alone me. He winks though and tells me he's found his prince, before looking serious again in case I'm still mad at him. I ask about Dasha, how she is. He doesn't know, doesn't remember her, her elegant figure wading through the seas. I remember her, her laced arms, her accessories like works of art, water filling the embroidered holes in her sleeves. I order a glass of red wine from a passing man with a tray.

'Where's your horse?' I ask Aleksandar.

'What? Sorry . . . I don't . . .'

'Never mind.'

Fab returns, whirls his chair a quick 360, and sits down with a shared-around smile, giving it to each of us individually before letting it come to rest on his face while he adjusts the position of his napkin until the grin slowly fades. I don't ask about Zlat but I find out anyway. He's moved to London to study a PhD, with his wife and young child. I start imagining it but then I stop and thankfully the wine arrives. I blur myself into the middle-distance. What does Frankfurt even mean? I spent a week here once sleeping on a mattress on some guy's floor while my friend slept in his folded-out sofa bed alongside him and her six-year-old son, and her and the Frankfurter did their best not to inadvertently have sex with each other in front of the child. Other than that, I don't remember a thing about this city, not one image remains. Yet here I am again. Fab's lived here his whole life, he says. So it must be real. 'Come on,' he says, 'we'll show you around.'

They take me through the motions over the next few days: bars, parks, buildings with step-facades that make me think of mechanical figurines walking comically up and down, town squares, churches, equestrian monuments, museums, enormous beers, wide roads, municipal buildings. I feel safe, gathered like a pack of cards, pressed together until all my edges align then wrapped neatly with a band and placed into a warm trouser pocket. Mostly, I just listen to their shared English, the delicate phrasing, the sculpting of the letters. I have a vague pressure in my head, uniform and low-lying, yet persistent as dark-grey blanket clouds. Sometimes when Aleksandar speaks directly to me I find I haven't heard the first few paragraphs; he comes into focus already in the full flow of a story, his outline sharpens, his lips, his teeth. I'm stepping through dense fog searching for the tip of my outstretched hand.

Fab's there but I'm not trying. I haven't asked him anything about himself. I sip soup and suck the sog off strips of bread in Turkish takeaways. He smiles warmly at me, I smile tiredly at him. I open my mouth to speak. Close it again. Aleksandar looks so happy; he's working remotely for a small Croatian company buying and selling the rights to digital images, Fab is a sous chef, and they are holding hands across the paper napkins on the table. I think about Blaze's hand and Sandra's hand and the handles of my plastic buckets. I think about the mist curling itself around the tree legs on the Wolfville hillsides or blowing smoke rings into its spartan coves. I think about the note I wrote on the perforated page, tiny peninsulas of paper hanging off like desperate entrails. I imagine Blaze telling his parents how excited he was about me, how he was going to reorganise the house, spruce up the garden, how they had to take the dog so I could really feel at home there. I imagine him clearing a bookshelf for me, emptying the loft, cleaning out the recesses of his wardrobe; building up to that day on the beach, proud and determined, satisfied and almost complete. I remember my childhood, how it went on and on and nothing really happened. I remember flickers of activity, week-long summer vacations, a few family members here and there getting together to celebrate an annual something or other. But mostly I remember building towers of cards on the dining-room table and teaching myself to juggle for entire two-month-long summer holidays, or hitting a ball against a kerb, waiting for it to return, and then hitting it against the kerb again. My childhood was grey, asphalt on asphalt, patches it's thought no one will pay attention to, but you do, you notice; it's inside you, the poor quality of the roads. The latest cultural novelty pasted clumsily into the cracks of the decade prior: a Tamagotchi, a heat-sensitive T-shirt, a mobile phone. Like new roads poured out onto inefficient dirt tracks, like staples over the shredded corners of previously stapled paper piles. I wasn't able to touch anything while it was still hot and malleable; a childhood spent waiting on the sidelines until the volatile liquid became stubborn and solid and pointless and old again. I remember waiting for my turn to speak, and then, when it came, being too scared to make a noise. I remember going about unnoticed and drifting, like the tide flowing in and out of ten-a-penny rock pools. Displacement, the head going under the expanding surface. Once upon a time there was a crash, an explosion, the plates rubbed against each other, fashions changed, hopeful plans were made for a collective future. Then, like exiting flood-water, I just sort of slowly ebbed away. I imagine Blaze crumbling earthward, a demolished tower in the aftermath of my most recent event. I stir a strip of bread around in the bowl of my unfinished lentil soup.

I'm kissing someone in a nightclub. I look at the watch on the arm of the man I'm holding and it is almost 4 a.m and I have no idea how I got here. I look for Aleksandar or Fab or Blaze or anyone but there is nobody, only tons of accidental bodies doing accidental things to each other on a dancefloor that happens to be in the way. 'Waltzing Matilda' starts playing and the crowd goes wildish and the man I'm apparently with whispers something in my ear about going

DISTANT HILLS

to Iceland or Greenland, how he feels a calling for the iceflats, the tundras, how man against nature, how elements, how survival, how discovering what you are made of, how marathon running. I tell him to get over himself, that he won't find anything there apart from whichever aspects of his personality he already spends too much time looking at and the justification to start that blog he's always dreamed of starting that no one but his mum will ever read. He looks at me like I haven't finished speaking but I have so I walk away from him and stumble around the climbing frame of bodies until I find a heap of clothes in a corner and start to look for anything that might be my coat but the hunt gets a bit much and I fall asleep.

It is daylight when somebody plucks me from that nest and stands me up on my own two feet. I leave without my coat, fumbling through central Frankfurt, trying not to make eye-contact with any of the more finalised people coming my way. Rashly, I call England, I hear the ringtone of what might be a parent, I hang up again. I call Aleksandar. He asks me just what the fuck is going on with me, tells me he is working and asks can I pick up some food for lunch if I am planning to head back to his place any time soon.

I start walking in the direction I think Aleksandar's house is in; too dizzy to get on any form of public transport or have anyone staring directly at my face. I pass the smells of shops and bakeries, I want it all, but instead I am sick in an unpopulated side street. I call Kathy. I tell her I am back in Europe and I haven't slept and I ask if she remembers that time we went camping in Scotland and the tent pole snapped and the rain and she asks me what the fuck am I doing back in Europe and where have I been actually and why hasn't she heard from me. I hang up. That wasn't what I had in mind at all. I pick up bread from a local chain store; I pick up soup. I worry about the smell that is no doubt trailing me in such a confined space and try to smile wholesomely, handing over the cash from as large a distance as my arms and back can provide. I leave quickly without turning around or showing my teeth. A man starts walking alongside me, asking me where I am from, did I have a good night, would I like to grab a coffee. He tells me his son is called Elmo and he loves my country and when I say I don't have time for a coffee he writes down his email address on the top margin of the newspaper he is carrying and rips it off and gives it to me. I walk down whichever road I think he is least likely to be taking—a plan that works out eventually. We hug goodbye with all the grease and smoke that is layering our unchanged clothing, and he finally leaves.

I can't face Aleksandar. I am dreading the approach of where he sits behind his computer screen. The tread of the pavement reminds me of the times I haven't lived through and the places I haven't been. Every step is a minor earthquake in the caverns of my brain. My insides are hollow, brittle, stripped back to the plaster, wide and unrenovated, with huge empty window frames. My vision fills with neon dots spinning in tiny fractal-like formations about multiple centres: a peep-show of pressure that, while vicing my thought patterns, is also beautiful in its sheer galactic detail.

Truth is I don't want to be anywhere at all. Since my twenty-first birthday, I've been approaching my life like a supermarket-reward scheme, saving and storing and then trying to eke out the good stuff for as long as possible before the coupons expire. My life is the shape of a slide: one near-vertical climb, hard and focused, that mainly involves concentrating on the task at hand while waiting to slip down the other side and take in the views. That long downward slope eventually trailing off into a calm and disappointing flatness in which I hope I won't be asked too many questions. Lying on the floor for months at a time, absolute stasis, until my legs creak apart and I go out and find a job again. My body is an ISA, full of potential energy, waiting to be released.

It is this wave-shape of existence that decides my moves. I am as monotonous and bland as the ocean—small peaks of interest, distant mountains that germinate and deplete. A white sheet flung up, spread out, pulled taut—and crumpled nightly by my inconsistent dreams. I grab at the human driftwood that passes me by, on trains, in temporary-employment recruitment-agency waiting rooms, in the bottlenecks of bars. Nothing holds fast, nothing stays. In the same way that stickers eventually peel off manufactured surfaces, in the same way that posters eventually curl away from walls.

Distance is in fact distance, despite what the internet would have us believe. There is distance enough between myself and the tree across the street, whose leaves I do not hear move in the equally inaudible wind.

I close my eyes. Finger the unvalidated tram ticket in my trouser pocket. There was the time in Bulgaria when the inspector got on, in plain clothes, and out of his pocket whipped a portable, quick-release, snap-button inspecting jacket. We hadn't paid, we weren't convincing enough in pretending not to understand the gist of what he was trying to say. The tram was packed, the doors were closed, the heat was leaking in. I remember the tram coming to a halt, the hiss of the doors decompacting, and a man's arm like a drop-down barrier between the inspector and us. *Run*, he said, and jabbed his head hard to the side. To the open doors and the gummy waves of heat twisting up from the concrete. And run we did, through the stuttering rows of traffic, past the floor-based stalls selling colourful tights and triple-packs of underpants in hexagonal underground stations, and back out into the casino-lined array. I want simple instructions, imploring eyes, the thrill of the chase.

Last time I saw Kathy's dad, he told me I should grow up, that he was surprised I hadn't bought myself a house yet, hadn't got myself a husband. He said I should grow up and then went on to tell me how much approximately each of his offspring earns. He's a retired business-owner, paints landscapes—trees, ponds, breathtaking sunsets—there are no reflections in the water.

I want to be wholly without context, limitations shoved to the bottom of my backpack. I want to push the bag into one of the station's many lockers and just leave. When you travel, you start off as a name on a ticket, a reservation number, mysterious and vague, before you form into the sound of a bell on a reception desk, or the tinkle of a well-baited door opening, rattling closed again. You are a pastel drawing, smudged into focus by the desk staff rubbing their eyes awake. You step into the dorm, the new guy, the maybe. But the second you speak, your possibilities rapidly dissolve and you start to morph back into the one thing you always were.

You can fight it. I have fought it. I've shed my skin as the naked wanderers did under the burn of the mid-American, mid-

discovered rays. I've ripped the friends off the skin of my arms, stopped replying to emails. I've deleted whole folders of digital photographs, by either the destination or the year. One right-click, one left-click, empty the bin, it all goes away. There is a kind of power in deleting your history. Maybe you end up with nothing, but better to have a little control over the proceedings, as you'll likely end up with nothing either way.

'You stink,' Aleksandar tells me, confirming what I already imagined must have been the case. I don't have much else to add, so I just kind of sit there stirring a tiny spoon around the inside of a cup of coffee I probably won't drink anyway. Aleksandar busies himself around my location at the centrally located kitchen table, stacking up dishes and putting them in their place, grabbing cutlery by the bundle and dealing it into its corresponding groove in the drawer-held plastic inlay.

'I'm leaving tomorrow,' I say. 'I booked a flight. So, I'll be out of your way. Thanks though, it's been really great seeing you again.'

He doesn't ask where I'm going. I'm quite sure he doesn't even turn around to acknowledge my words, although maybe I am not paying enough attention. Maybe I'm stirring the coffee and staring at the handle of the tiny spoon, wishing it would break and surprise me. Or maybe I'm blocking out his face in case it's showing me pity or love or, worse, complete disinterest, and it's better if you stay away from those things. Better to stay in the main room of the party, where the music is loud and the drink is plentiful and nobody is saying anything they might regret later, or if they do, the listener is too bombarded with noise and exaggerated taps on the shoulders to be sure they even remember the speaker's name.

Maybe I didn't say the words out loud. Maybe the back of Aleksandar's head is waiting for me to say something a little more convincing. Like I'll stay and live here. That we'll be neighbours soon, or, at the very least, friends who will always have each other's backs and laugh at each other's frequent mistakes and remind each other of the stupid shit we once did—under the thin veil of teasing, but really to let each other know what wise and mature people we think we now are. How far we've come. How everything is forgiven and our fingers are forever wrapping around each other like adjoining tree branches on the far side of passing years. How nothing is my fault and all of this just sort of occurred.

But he doesn't even look at me. Aleksandar doesn't even turn around. He just goes on heating his pasta and chopping up vegetables and adding them to the pan in which he will eventually create his sauce. I am crushing the uncrushable tiny spoon in my poor hand. The undersides of my knuckles have never proved anything. I'm leaving. Aleksandar is done.

I'm going to go where I don't know anyone and start again, and this time I'll have the answers prepared. When they ask me about my family, I will not falter. I will not have their eyes looking at me like maybe I should be doing something about the situation, like maybe I could put in the legwork, like maybe I could jack up the rusty car that will eventually come crashing back down. I'll start again, career too; I'll meet like-minded individuals and when they ask what I do I'll make it sound cohesive: retail-based, customer-focused, driven, loves new challenges, adaptable, immersive, skills across the board. I'll find something, someone will open a door.

DISTANT HILLS

I'm going upstairs to pack because I can't stay here if he won't look at me. I should have known when he fled after Else's sudden decline. I should have known then that he couldn't pull out enough reserves to help a friend in need, couldn't take the time to soothe the waves for anyone other than himself. I should have known long before then not to put stock in anyone, not to take my foot off the pedal, not to take my eyes off the shore. And I'm down on the ground, fists in the Frankfurt sand of Aleksandar's rotten rental kitchen, sifting the cracks of tiles for gems, amber, fossils, stone, ticket stubs, when the waves come in, when the tide creeps up hours too soon. I took my eyes off the lighthouse, and the black-and-white squares are shifting beneath my body like desert dunes. Blaze's face moves across the swarming tiles—G9 to F8. Check. Checkmate. The swell comes and I'm under. If you hesitate, you're gone. Keep your feet firm and surrender your limbs to the rushes and sways, like those tubular wind socks with great smiling cartoon faces that dance wild and high outside advancing gastro-pubs and independent service stations along the busy roads that link somewhere to somewhere else again.

XX.

I'M IN FRANKFURT Airport, staring at my rucksack on the ground against the cubicle door beneath the coat hanging from the hook as I wait for anything to appear at all.

I splash water on my face. I pick up my rucksack, swinging it onto my left shoulder with enough momentum to send it across my back and toward my other arm. I clip the belly strap in place. All parts of the process—the buckle, the texture of my jacket, the zip, the click—feeling a little more solid and certain than usual. I look at myself in the mirror with no particular goal—expression neutral—and learn nothing. I unlock the door, step into the placeless tumult of the airport interior—passengers like invisible crisscrossing laser beams ready to strike if you step out too soon.

Acknowledgements

I am eternally grateful to the teachers of Salford University who have helped me along the way over the years: Scott Thurston, Ursula Hurley, the invaluable Paul Haywood, Karen Lyons, and Helen Sargeant (for telling me I was not a painter).

I would like to thank so many of my friends for encouraging and/or indulging me at so many points in time . . . they know who they are.

Thanks, in particular, to those who have helped and read this manuscript at various stages of its life cycle: Rachel Martin, Karen Kendrick, David Martin, Shimanto, Enrique (as ever), and Sabrina Stephan.

And a huge thank you to Andersen Prunty and Atlatl Press for giving this book a home.

Other **Atlatl Press** Books

Murder House by C.V. Hunt
No Music and Other Stories by Justin Grimbol
Elaine by Ben Arzate
Bird Castles by Justin Grimbol
Fuck Happiness by Kirk Jones
Impossible Driveways by Justin Grimbol
Giraffe Carcass by J. Peter W.
Shining the Light by A.S. Coomer
Failure As a Way of Life by Andersen Prunty
Hold for Release Until the End of the World
by C.V. Hunt
Die Empty by Kirk Jones
Mud Season by Justin Grimbol
Death Metal Epic (Book Two: Goat Song Sacrifice)
by Dean Swinford
Come Home, We Love You Still by Justin Grimbol
We Did Everything Wrong by C.V. Hunt
Squirm With Me by Andersen Prunty
Hard Bodies by Justin Grimbol
Arafat Mountain by Mike Kleine
Drinking Until Morning by Justin Grimbol
Thanks For Ruining My Life by C.V. Hunt
Death Metal Epic (Book One: The Inverted Katabasis)
by Dean Swinford
Fill the Grand Canyon and Live Forever by Andersen Prunty
Mastodon Farm by Mike Kleine
Fuckness by Andersen Prunty
Losing the Light by Brian Cartwright
They Had Goat Heads by D. Harlan Wilson
The Beard by Andersen Prunty

Lightning Source UK Ltd.
Milton Keynes UK
UKHW011335070621
385079UK00005B/1556